DREAMS OF S

Iron Dragon Bool
By Tim Niederriter

Book Description

This is a work of fiction People, places, events, and situations are the product of the author's imagination. Any similarity to actual people, places, and events is purely coincidental.

Dragons are real. The race to control them has begun.

Leoten carries the spirit of an Iron Dragon in his mind but doesn't know what that means yet. When he receives a letter from an imprisoned friend his new mission becomes clear.

Dispatched to rescue Nerida from a dangerous Arctic base, Leoten has to make new alliances and use every resource available to achieve his goal.

She knows how to forge new dragons and he knows the world needs them.

"Dreams of Static" is the second book in the Iron Dragon series, and the sequel to "They Have the Scent." If you like a little strangeness and plenty of spies with your magic and dragons, start at the beginning.

Prologue

The mountain's cold brought the dragon's mind closer to the surface. Leoten sat cross-legged on the threshold of his tent and exhaled a misty breath. Despite the chill that crept up his bare arms to the fresh knife scar on his right shoulder exposed by the cut of his sleeveless shirt.

The dragon's peaceful presence touched his consciousness. Serene warmth spread through him from his head to his heart and then to his extremities.

The sun crossed its zenith but he stayed with the spirit of the dragon in meditation. He distanced himself from the sensations of hunger, thirst, and cold.

At last, he rose to cook dinner at the dragon's urge. He struck a match and lit the fire that began to heat the pot of chicken and vegetable broth. He turned to the long-legged great strider that waited dutifully beside his tent. The creature dipped a long, scaly snout, and ate the chunks of meat and tomato he brought in his cupped palms.

He only dimly noticed the sound of heavy feet that drew closer to where he ate on the mountain side.

As the sun began to sink, a lone strider approached Leoten's camp, carrying both an old friend and a message from command. She told him the contents of the short letter were urgent.

He took the letter into the tent where he'd camped and opened it at once.

The letter's first line sent a thrill down Leoten's spine that outmatched the cold of the mountain air.

"Agent Seol, regarding the matter of the Iron Dragon," he read, "Our contact has requested your assignment to this mission by name. She says you've met."

He lowered the paper from before his eyes. The flicker of the gas lantern in the tent made the words dance upon the page, but there was no mistake as to what it said. Leoten unfolded his legs and then stood. He put on his outer coat and then ducked out the flap of the tent.

Silhouetted against the setting sun, the form of two great woolly-haired striders loomed over the messenger who'd just delivered the letter to him on the mountainside. One of the striders belonged to her and one to Leoten.

"What's the word?" The messenger stood with her arms folded, back to the wind that blew cold off the mountaintop.

Leoten pulled on his boots. "They've sent me a mission, Yoka."

She raised a brow. "That so? You ready to head back?"

"I think so." He began to break down the camp. Yoka helped him pack up the tent and load everything onto Leoten's saddle. Both of them mounted their steeds.

They rode a half-mile to the spot the trail up the slope ended and then turned to descend the mountain.

"Can you tell me where they're sending you?" she asked.

"Not in the long run. But our first stop is Koria. From there, I can't say."

"Understood." Yoka rolled her dark eyes. "I'll learn my part when the time comes."

"That's how the agency likes it, right?"

"You've been out of the game for a few months, though I suppose not much has changed."

They crossed an old, stone bridge over a narrow river that rushed with snow melt.

"It will," said Leoten.

"What will?"

"If my guess is right," he said. "Everything."

Yoka laughed. "Don't be so dramatic. We've got three days' ride ahead of us, you know?"

Leoten half-smiled. "Fine, but I can't tell you what the letter contained."

"I know, but it'll be good to have you back, Leoten."

"It's only been six months."

"Longer than that, because you didn't tell me about your unplanned sabbatical after the incident in Volskorod."

He scratched his neck. "Sorry. I just needed to meditate on what happened."

"Seems it affected you, unlike most missions."

He nodded.

Yoka guided her strider to the edge of a slope overlooking a narrow valley. She gazed passed the gnarled trees and rocks that surrounded the tiny village below, situated along a mostly dry riverbed. Her eyes fixed on each new light as they began to come on in the houses below. The snows must still be mostly caught up in the highlands. "You'll have plenty of time to think as long as you're among the living."

"Life and death might be a coin toss for us sometimes," said Leoten, "but it's a coin we must flip anyway."

"Was that poetry or philosophy? I know you enjoy both."

"You also know I'm no good at either."

"True," said Yoka. "Doesn't stop you from trying, though."

They descended into the valley, then crossed the river on a small bridge in the woods north of the village. Such a remote trail made them less noticeable to the locals.

Their ride continued through the TCR's heartland, toward the city of Koria. Spring in the southeastern nation of the Triumvirate of Custodial Republics brought green life to burst forth in every direction. Insects buzzed and frogs croaked all along the roadside until the twilight became full dark lit only by the stars. Leoten and Yoka camped the night before continuing north in the morning.

They kept on until they reached the city on the third day.

• • • •

CHAPTER 1
Two Weeks Later

The crab boat churned through the icy waters north of the island nation of Otrusia. Leoten waited for the crew to haul them into view of the smaller island, Sarga, about fifty miles from the Otrusian coast. He gazed at the clear blue sky and knew he'd need to wait for dusk to begin infiltration. His seal-cloth mimic suit still lay folded in the trunk between his feet.

Inside the trunk, he also carried a large caliber pistol, a silencer for the gun, and six capsules that contained fungal communication sprouts. When combined with the metal thimbles and receivers he wore on two of his fingers, each sprout could connect him by voice to the team on the TCR light cruiser that idled in the water to the southwest, a short distance over the horizon.

Leoten's immediate superiors in the agency had planted part of the fungal pile from which the sprouts had been plucked to allow them to stay in contact with him. The mission itself called for one operative in the field. The Otrusian Research labs beside the island of Sarga offered heavy security, especially.

The local crabber captain turned toward him as the crew prepared the steel nets to cast for their prey. "You a strange young man, Mister Red."

"Stranger than your usual crew, Captain Holt?"

Holt grinned. One of his front teeth was cracked like the Pirate Tarok from the Otrusian national epic poem. Leoten wondered, not for the first time if the captain recognized the resemblance. Holt nodded. "Yah."

Leoten smiled. "I like to think I've lived an interesting life."

Holt scoffed. "It get more interesting once you get to Idraster. Or it end there."

"One way or the other..." Leoten looked to the west, off the bow of the boat.

A small tower with sheet metal walls rose from the water perhaps two miles off the tip of Sarga's rocky shore. The tower looked modern, complete with relay branches, pile vines, and an array of searchlights that jutted from the rounded peak.

Yet, the tower climbed from the water which seemed to flatten for a short distance around the base of the structure. Leoten's briefing had included the intelligence that more of Idraster base was underwater than above, hence the warm mimic suit they'd given him for the swim. He'd go in through the coldest route and count on his mission case's ability to withstand the water.

•   •   •   •

LEOTEN SWAM WITH THE case, tucking the bag over his shoulder. The bag was made of the same material as his wetsuit. He swam stroke over stroke through the icy waters, his head completely covered in seal-hide survival gear, lest his ears freeze off in the cold. Otrusia was an unforgiving environment to those who braved its waters.

He reached the grate on the underside on the side of Idraster base, where the metallic walls slanted upward at a more than vertical angle. The angle left visible only a slim hint of the port in the base's side. It could have been a torpedo tube in a warship, but such things were usually not seen in battles, except when larger forces went to war. No doubt, there existed some kind of engineered creature that would swim in and out of here.

As Leoten proceeded into the dark tunnel just barely wide enough for him to swim, he noted the slight flickers of light ahead. After just seconds in the tunnel, he poked his head out of the water at the end of the tunnel.

Near where he floated, a number of sea runners were basking line on a metallic plate within the base. This must be where the sea runners used for messenger forays and other excursions were kept to nest. They resembled large sea lions but with more developed forelimbs. Those front flippers looked nearly long enough to match the great striders ridden overland. Their webbed fins and aquatic body shapes left him with doubt that they could compete with most normal beasts for long on a journey overland. Each sea runner also had a pair of wickedly hooked talons on the backs of their shorter, rear fins.

Leoten might have feared them, but for the peace of the dragon and his confidence in his mind eater abilities. His calm subdued the creatures' curiosity and kept them from lashing out as he drew closer. No matter their training, the animals mustn't expect to meet a human in their habitat.

Despite the presence of breathable air in the cavernous chamber, Leoten kept his breather mask on, as he proceeded past the cluster of sea runners. He reached the iron ladder that the base's personnel used to access the pool. He climbed until he reached the top, where rust melded into the metal wall of the base. He peered over the top in a cautious, survey in case of guards on duty. He noted a discarded cigarette butt on the floor. With curiosity, he crested the top of the wall and approached the fallen piece of litter.

He crouched and removed his glove then turned his hand over, to detect any heat that wafted from the remnant. It was still warm, but not much more than a spark in the cold room where his breath misted before him. If a guard had discarded it recently, the cigarette would be cold. *He must be near*, Leoten thought. He reached out with his mind.

The guard patrolled nearby, just a bit further down the passage. Leoten backed away from cigarette butt, and off into one side of the chamber where the sea runners lurked below. Normal humans without mind eater abilities or other sensory magic like the spirit seer he'd encountered once before would have difficulty hiding from the trained runners' attention. Sea runners were similar to the striders and other creatures created over the centuries, by humanity from the remnants of the dragons from the past.

The goddesses had left them behind, or so the great books told. The Triumvirate and many other nations relied on the power of the three ancient goddesses, but very few understood them and Leoten wasn't among that number. He barely believed in the deities themselves, but their handiwork was obvious. Humanity had shaped the world with their castoff abilities, which remained as obvious testament to some kind of intelligence in the world around them.

Designing creatures was the purpose of this base, and the sea runners were rare outside of Otrusia. *Who knew if perhaps these had been modified further in recent years?*

Leoten approached the patrolling guard, keeping his footsteps soft and timed to the sentry's movements. In silence, he focused to activate the tattoo seal on his hand to summon his bonded signature knife from its shrine far away. The seal burned hot and the knife dropped into his grip, slightly curved with a sharp edge, and a sharper point. He didn't move. He didn't mean to take the guard's life but he would need to be ready in case he was noticed so close to the foe. Before the guard could turn, Leoten wrapped arms around his neck from behind. He coked the blocked flow from the guard's head. The sentry was unconscious before he hit the floor.

Leoten dragged the unconscious man just to rest by the cigarette butt.

He put a hand to the guard's temples and drained what little urge the man had to waken himself and stand. Unlike some mind-eaters, Leoten didn't become much stronger when he fed on thoughts, but he could be more aggressive than others with his powers. He couldn't do much harm with his abilities, except to slow people down or put them to sleep with greater effort. In this case, the guard was already unconscious. To keep him that way by draining one impulse at a time proved easy. Leoten decided to let the guard sleep the encounter off for at least half an hour. Once he felt the sentry dreaming, Leoten left his side and proceeded up the stairs to the higher levels of the base. He made his way through a few narrow square-cornered metallic corridors, toward the partially submerged place where the tower above connected to the underwater supports of the complex below.

These passages would've been at home on a military ship. They certainly felt narrow enough for such tight confines. Leoten was average in height, but strong and steady enough for most physical combat. Still, others could outstrip him in raw muscular power.

Leoten started the search for any internal lab that might house experiments like those his target would be assigned. Yet, despite the clues from Nerida's letter, he found interpreting the layout of the base difficult. *Yes*, he thought, *Nerida is still alive. She helped create the first Iron Dragon, and she was the key to re-creating it.*

At that thought, another sensory impulse chimed in the back of Leoten's mind. No words followed, but a thought leaped forth from acute imagery. The visual belonged to a red-haired woman that some might call beautiful. Yet, her true strength was in her mind, not in her face or muscles. She was a magus of flame, who had helped engineer both the first Iron Dragon in Otrusia and the second in Volskorod.

Leoten helped her as much as he could, but both dragons had been destroyed. Only the mind of the second still lived within him.

He approached the gateway that led to a larger chamber within the center of Idraster base. He must be on a higher level now because he could see sunlight slanting through the water in shades of orange and filtering through windows in the ceiling. The skylights offered up a chance at the sky, but the clouds looked ready to close up the heavens before night fell.

Leoten looked into the room beyond the hatchway door.

Within, he found who he'd hoped to see. Clad in a white coat, Nerida leaned into a tight conversation with a wispy-haired man and a slender, dark-haired woman on the other side of a metal table. The three of them all in their white lab coats were flanked on all sides by a squad of Otrusian Guards in dark blue-green uniforms. Each of the eight soldiers carried a full-sided automatic rifle as well as a pistol at the hip and no doubt a combat blade or other close-quarters weapon concealed elsewhere.

Each of them might be a match for Leoten in the battle if aware of him. He possessed no illusions that despite his skill, magic, and Bruise training, he could take eight soldiers at once in a direct fight

Nerida and the others still hadn't seen him. He wished he could reach out like a spirit magus might allow. If his powers could touch Nerida's thoughts, then getting her to separate from the rest would be simple. The art of projecting his mind-eater abilities had been a secret he'd failed to learn in the Temple of Colors when he'd infiltrated that strange place for the Triumvirate.

He flattened against the wall within the passage. He'd find a way to retrieve Nerida if he knew the resources and experiments within the base better. She'd written a letter for him to read and managed to send it somehow from this forbidding base on the north end of the world. She and the dragon's mind within him wanted the same thing as Leoten..

Another Iron Dragon must be made.

They'd see more of those majestic creatures rise from the depths of myth and history to join humanity in the present. And yet, he feared what their enemies, the shoddok from beyond the world, would attempt at every step of that plan. They wanted nothing more than to see the dragons remain extinct.

Nerida could make the difference in creating a brighter future. Otrusia might be allied with the TCR now, but if they tried to keep Nerida against her will, Leoten would treat them as enemies.

He crouched and peered around the corner with minimal parts exposed to sight on the other side. Leoten spotted a familiar figure. She wore a black seal suit and armored vest with no obvious weapons. She turned away from him. He had to act. Yet, he knew from experience that the tall woman could surprise him.

"Sarah Hanzioni," he breathed, then darted forward, signature knife in hand. She'd betrayed them back and Volskorod, but still he didn't plan on using the blade if she didn't force the need.

He closed with the Otrusian agent. She spun as he drew close, moving too fast for him to take her down without a fight. She had at least one other thing in common with him beyond their time and Volskorod.

A short blade materialized in her hand, appearing from the bond on her sleeve under her sleeve. She grasped the handle and blocked his signature knife. The force drove her back a step but didn't faze her beyond that.

"You're early." She sneered at him and her lips twitched.

"What you talking about?" asked Leoten. "Did you know I was coming?"

"Of course," said Sarah. "We caught Nerida after she sent that letter. She couldn't keep her lips shut forever."

"You're better at counterintelligence than I thought."

"Of course," said Sarah. She smiled at him. "Nothing personal, Leoten. But I think it's time you left, empty-handed as ever."

Leoten grunted but said nothing else in reply. They clashed for a moment but with her longer blade she'd quickly gain the edge over him. She made her blade's reach more valuable than Leoten's larger build by retreating as he pressed her. When he hesitated, she forced him backward with the point of the sword. He avoided being cut, but at the cost of dropping his mission bag with the case inside.

Sarah prowled closer, languid and calm. Before Leoten could attempt another strike, she tapped her ear with a thimble that capped one finger, and her chin with the one opposite. Her local fungal communications pile, no doubt.

She said, "Alert, security. We have an intruder." She looked at him as she removed the finger from her chin. "Leoten, you'd best leave now or you won't be able to escape."

"I have a mission," said Leoten.

"So do I." Sarah's eyes flashed as a pair of guards emerged from a set of doors on opposite sides of the passageway, swinging through the hatches with rifles in hand. Idraster's security troopers closed with Leoten fast. Despite his training in the Bruise Regiment, he refused to strike out like a hornet with the intent to fight to the death.

He put up his hands and nodded to Sarah. "Well played."

She nodded but said nothing more in return. The guards dragged him down the unnatural metal hallway. He banished his knife before they could take it from them.

"Keep his hands tied," said Sarah as he is. The guards roughly marched him into what appeared to be some kind of board room, not a cell. The furnishings surprised Leoten.

"What are we doing here?" he asked.

"Well, you're going to explain to me who you are." A man with thick black hair and wearing a ballistic-plated Otrusian Guard uniform and rimless glasses stepped into the room. The man carried no weapon, but he could have some armament bonded to him.

"My name is Red," said Leoten. "And yours?"

"Roy." The man patted his chest with his palm. "Roy Chenn, chief of security."

• • • •

CHAPTER 2

The security chief Roy Chenn paced in front of the table. "So you're Nerida's heroic rescuer," he shook his head. "It's a shame what happened in Volskorod. I knew Henry Klaudenn. He was a friend."

"And yet you keep Nerida here against her will?" said Leoten.

"I do my job," said Roy. "But I'm afraid I've got extra pressure on me today. We're under inspection. And that means we're all to be on our best behavior, especially when there's a spy infiltrating the base."

Leoten quirked a small smile. "I wouldn't want to cause you any trouble. Our nations are allies, after all."

"I somehow doubt you feel as you say." Roy smirked. "But I like you already, despite your lack of a name. What was it that Sarah called you?"

Leoten shrugged theatrically. "You heard it, didn't you? I won't repeat it for you."

"You don't have to," said Roy. "As far as I'm concerned, you're just an operative here to disrupt our experiments. The station chief would tell me I should just have you shot. But I'm curious."

"Curious about what?" asked Leoten.

"I'm curious as to how you got in here so quietly. We found the guard you knocked out, but he was barely even bruised. I'd I know you if got into through a sealed door. That leaves the3 the sea runner nest, but those creatures would tear an ordinary intruder to shreds. So what are you?"

Heavy footsteps approached from the door, clearly audible over the hum of the station's machines.

"Full of surprises," said Leoten. "But you may not want to wait for the next one." He nodded toward the door behind Roy. "Is that your station chief?"

"It is," said Roy, turning and saluting the heavy-set man who stepped into the room, flanked by two more soldiers from his Otrusian guard unit.

"So this is our intruder?" the chief asked. "I'm impressed, made so far into the base without anyone detecting you but you picked the wrong woman to mess with. As far as taking out our sentries."

"She got my number," said Leoten. "But I have to ask, I'm not an enemy, so. I'm from the TCR. You might as well come clean as to what you doing on this station. I don't see a sign of another Iron Dragon here, nor a distillery for blood-related research."

"We have other ways of making dragons in Otrusia," said the station chief. "Though, another Iron Dragon would still be the pinnacle at the moment. We are working on one but not here. I suppose your intelligence didn't tell you that."

"To be honest, I haven't had much of a chance to look around."

"I should think not come close is the station chief." Now you pestered," he laughed. "I'm afraid Roy, here's been too nice to you. I'm going to have to take you and execute you myself, aren't I?"

"I don't think your government would appreciate that," said Leoten. "But you'll do what you want to do."

"Oh, I will," said the station chief. "Red."

The two Otrusian guards each clapped a hand on one of Leoten's arms.

Leoten smiled as he wiped away the thoughts of the guards on either side of him. They stepped backward, then slumped to the floor slowly, their backs supporting each other on the way down. He'd devoured their will to stand. His hands still bound, he slipped under the table to avoid anyone else shooting at him.

With his back against the wall, he summoned his signature knife and cut his hands free. The rope fell to the floor behind him.

"Nice trick," said Roy.

"I just want to talk," said Leoten.

"Kill this man," said the station chief. "He's resisting, despite my attempt to keep his blood off my hands."

One of the Otrusian base guards rounded the corner with a rifle in his hands. He caught the blade of Leoten's signature knife in his knee. The man went down clutching his wounded joint. The knife appeared back in Leoten's hand.

"A signature knife is an unusual weapon," said Crane as his footfalls prowled around the other side of the table. "But it also gives you away. You're that bruise, regiment veteran, aren't you?"

"You got me," said Leoten.

He turned the corner, ready to hurl the knife end over end at the station chief. The chief hesitated, eyes locked on something over Leoten shoulder.

Leoten glanced back, to see the guard he'd wounded contorting, shifting and meet and warping in shape and form. I didn't do that," he said. He said under his breath. "What the hell is going on."

The man shifted and moved like a contortionist. He scuttled to the wall like a bizarre shellfish and then bashed his head against the metal.

One of the other guards ran to hold the man back from crushing his skull against the metal wall, while Roy looked around the room as the other Otrusian soldiers began to collapse one by one and fall to the floor.

"Chenn," said the station chief. "Get out of this room and find out what's going on. "Whatever is happening, he must have brought someone else with him."

Leoten shook his head. "I came here alone. Now, you've got a bigger problem than me."

He held the knife ready to throw at the station chief.

Crane gripped his pistol in both white-knuckled hands. "Damn you./" He must know that he couldn't raise the gun in time to keep Leoten's blade from killing him. "Roy," said the station chief. "Get out there and find out what's happening in my base."

Roy Chenn obeyed. He left the room of collapsed men and went disappeared into the passage outside the hatch.

Leoten listened to the sound of his footsteps succeed. He stared at the station chief. "I guess you must have other visitors."

The chief grunted and eased his finger off the trigger of his pistol.

A huge crashing sound burst from the passageway. Leoten's eyes narrowed but he kept his blade bare and aimed at the station chief.

"This isn't something you planned for?" Crane asked.

Leoten shook his head.

• • • •

CHAPTER 3

Leoten sprang to his feet before the station chief manged to straighten himself. The mass in the hall outside with another explosion rocked the hot side.

"You say you don't know what that is?" asked Chief Crane.

"I wish I did," said Leoten. "It would make things easier for me."

"Chief." Roy Chenn turned back to the door. "It's hell out here."

"Chenn," said Crane. "What the devil is going on out there?"

"By the goddesses, sir," said Chenn. "There's only one, but we can't stop him."

Someone screamed in the hall outside.

"Dammit," said the station chief.

"Look," said Leoten. "Whatever that thing is out there, he's worse than me."

"Tell that to the last TCR agent to try to attack this place," said the station chief. "When you meet them in the afterlife."

Leoten glared at Crane. "Weren't you going to try and kill me anyway?"

The station chief grimaced. "I wish I didn't have to," he said. "But with the inspectors here, and another attacker on base..." He bit his lip. "Damn it all!"

Roy Chenn ducked into the conference room, breathing hard. "Whoever this attacker is, he must be some kind of magus too powerful for ordinary men. My team is almost completely wiped out."

"Are you the only one left?" asked the station chief.

"Wakefield might still be alive," said Chenn. "But who knows for how much longer."

Leoten stepped forward. "I think I know what's happening."

"What do you think it is?" asked Roy Chenn.

"It might be a shoddok," said Leoten. "A kind of creature from beyond the world."

"Beyond the world?" said the station chief with a grunt. "How dare you spout such nonsense."

"The technology, the dragons could do many things we don't understand," said Leoten. "Nerida told me that."

"You know Nerida." Crane sucked his teeth. "Of course, she'd ask for someone she knew."

"Well," said Leoten. "I think I might be able to stop this if you let me out there."

"Fine," the station chief. "Get yourself killed for all I care. Just get out of here and stop interfering with our plans."

Leoten glanced at Roy Chenn. The security chief let him stand up and motioned him outside. He stepped into the hallway signature knife flipped upright and ready to throw.

Terrible laughter echoed down the hallway. Somehow, it sounded almost muted, as if coming from someplace muffled within a bag.

"Who's there?" Leoten scanned the smoky hallway. Debris and droplets of mist drifted from the ceiling as streams of water leaked in from above.

A lone figure stood in the hallway before him, and grinned with a wide mouth and pale visage, the only possible source of the laughter. The head was completely smooth, elongated over the back from the strangely cropped eyes and the impossibly wide vacuum-like mouth. The being had no ears or nose, but the creature whatever it was otherwise humanoid. The mouth opened in a ludicrously large smile, vast and fearsome. The fingers extended forward, related, like bones nearly bear of flesh, except with the tiniest threads of muscle.

"I see you dragon," said the creature.

The Dragon within Leoten seethed against his instincts. "You can tell it's here," said Leoten. "What are you?"

"I am from beyond," said the creature. "My name is Hargruss. And I have no need to share my secrets with mortals like you."

Leoten sprang forward, dagger in hand. He flipped the signature knife over and then released it. The blade straight tumbled twice and then flew straight toward the demon's face. Hargruss interposed his other hand to try and catch the weapon. The blade pierced the thin skin of the palm and came out the other side to stop inches from the creature's face.

Leoten called the signature knife and flip it into the throwing position, once more. Pinkish blood trailed from the blade.

"How crude," said Hargruss. "To strike so suddenly." The groaning bodies of the wounded guards littered the floor. The dust began to settle. More water began to rush into the chamber.

"How inconvenient," said Hargruss. "There is a danger here. I recognize you now dragon-keeper."

"How do you recognize me?" Leoten's brows bent inward.

"From the hotel," said the creature. "You remember the seal on the floor and the blood offering, don't you?"

"That was months ago," said Leoten. "Of course, I remember. I was supposed to save the people who were killed there."

"That was what brought me here," said the creature's soft sweet voice. "Too bad it didn't serve for the shoddok that summoned me. It didn't bind my will."

"So that was why he burned that page from the Book of Becoming when he killed them?" asked Leoten. "Just to summon you?"

"Yes," said Hargruss. "But that's all you will know." He stepped forward, languidly sweeping past the fallen bodies on the floor. His cloak was pale, almost gray, but only came up to his midsection. His chest and arms were fully exposed as if he'd planned for some kind of exotic costume party, rather than a combat mission. Yet, across his chest hung the strap of an unbonded blade's sheath.

Leoten grimaced at Hargruss. "Enough talk. Right." He summoned his dagger once more.

Hargruss darted forward to meet him. Before they collided, Roy Chenn stepped into the passage from a hatchway beside Leoten and delivered four bullets from his pistol into Hargruss.

"Down!" Roy shouted.

Hargruss swept his open palm in a wide arc, and a swift blast of force smashed Roy back through the doorway. Bullets pinged as they ricocheted off the walls around the conference room hatch. Leoten cringed against the doorframe and the telekinetic force of the strange magic didn't strike him. Roy found his sense and stumbled as he retreated into the conference room.

Leoten hurled his dagger, but Hargruss raised a hand and tossed the blade back through the air. The knife would've cut through Leoten's neck, but he returned it to the bond shrine with a twist of thought. He summoned the weapon back to his hand and found it clean of blood again.

"You are cunning with such a small trinket," said Hargruss. "But you can't stop me."

"What do you want?" asked Leoten.

"Nothing you need to know," said Hargruss as swept his hand back.

Water began to pour in from the ceiling and with the dismissive flick of the wrist, Hargruss hurled Leoten tumbling over and over down the passageway, through an open hatch, and across the floor of an empty barracks. He hit the wall with a cry of pain. The blow knocked the wind from his lungs. He would bruise for certain. His dagger clattered at his feet in the corridor just before him. He slid into a supine position with a grunt of what little breath he had left.

Hargruss stood over 30 meters away. That powerful throw had sent him skidding far. Yet, he seemed to have landed rather gently considering the momentum invovled. *Count yourself lucky.* As he blinked from the floor, a shadow detached from the inside passage and slipped toward Hargruss. Sarah. She leapt at the sorcerer with her sword in both hands.

Hargruss caught her by the throat.

As icy water poured around them, Hargruss turned his back on Leoten and marched the opposite way down the passage. He threw Sarah against the wall evidently uninterested in her as prey. She crumpled to the wet floor.

• • • •

CHAPTER 4

Leoten got to his feet group with a grunt and grimace. The storage room where he'd landed was vacant of other people and lit only dimly. Where ever he'd ended up, the battle in the hallway must be a large distraction for the guards. Regardless of why Hargruss had invaded the base, the terrifying alien sorcerer would draw most of the security forces to try to stop him.

"What can I do?" he asked himself.

He had to get his mission case, which must still be in the conference room. That resilient box contained all his communication supplies.

As Leoten got to his feet, Hargruss turned to look over his shoulder. Leoten stayed low and crept close to the wall so staying behind the doorframe of the chamber he'd been hurled into. The compartment in front of him was already filling with icy water and an emergency klaxon began to blare. The hatchway doors sealed halfway down the passage that was beginning to fill with water. Only daring provided the slender thread of hope that remained that he might be able to reach the conference room before those doors sealed him out.

The conference room might not have another way out of it, but to regain his chance at communicating with control, he had to try. He got to his feet and lurched forward with painful but swift steps. Leoten skirted what he could of the icy water on the floor before he lost any choice but to lunge through it to the conference room.

The security door had already halfway shut, but he spotted his mission case where it lay beside the table. Roy Chenn and the station chief were gone. Evidently, the two of them had known the time to exit the fight. Leoten saw no other way out of this conference room beyond the doors to the waterlogged passage he'd just entered through.

Leoten hurled himself out of the hatch just before it sealed. He landed in the pool of cold water in the hallway, on all fours. Luckily the case was still in its watertight bag.

He got his feet in the chill and rushed to the hallway. The bodies on the floor had begun to sink into the icy water. Sarah got to her feet slowly where Hargruss dropped her. Her sword was gone, banished back to wherever she kept the bonded weapon.

Leoten looked down at her. "Do you want my help?"

"Do you think I need you?" she hissed.

Hargruss turned his head toward them. "Neither of you wields any power that can stop me." The sorcerer grinned with a glint of teeth in his wide mouth. "And the two of you together will do no better."

"Perhaps," said Leoten under his breath. He grabbed Sarah by the arm and pulled her to her feet. They both passed through the passage door just before it closed to keep the water in the hallway. Leoten looked at Sarah. "You're lucky he didn't kill you."

She pushed him away. Her hands left bloodied prints on his shirt on his seal suit. "I still have to try to stop you from getting Nerida out of here," said Sarah. "She must not go back to the Triumvirate."

"Why not?" asked Leoten. "Seems to me your base is compromised."

"The project has to go on," said Sarah. "And we need Nerida for that."

"She doesn't want to be here," said Leoten. "That's why she wrote me that letter."

"I brought her here for a reason. We need to complete new dragons and we need to be able to stop the beings from beyond. I don't trust the Corporeum or the TCR. I only trust Otrusia. That's what I fight for."

"You have a chance now. To fight for something greater."

"Is that supposed to be poetic?" Sarah said. "Or just garbage?"

"Just words," said Leoten.

"Of course." She blinked and turned away from the passage door. "Don't follow me. If you do, I'll kill you."

Leoten waited for her to go and then took the opposite passage. He wasn't about to let her go completely, but he needed some time to reassess the situation.

Maybe, I need to contact Damaia on the ship. Perhaps she could send reinforcements.

Leoten looked into the tower's interior. From the bottom, a ladder led to the surface level, while the stairs went up the inside of the tower in the center of the base. There stood four men, all of them with heavy rifles. They wore black ballistic vests and heavy cloth face coverings. *They must not be guards,* thought Leoten. He readied his signature knife as he retreated around the corner.

One of the men laughed out loud. "Looks like we got a bond mage among us. That's our cue to move out, people."

Leoten wasn't ready to fight them yet. He ran across the hall and slammed into the hatch there. He twisted the security lock on the door and sealed himself into the room across the hall from the tower and the four soldiers. Hopefully, the hatch would hold against bullets if they chose to shoot at them. He held his breath, but the soldiers didn't shoot. Instead, he heard their feet move along the passage, following the path Sarah had taken. Apparently, they were also invaders. *Could they be working with Hargruss?*

Whoever they were, they must be less alien than the sorcerer, because they appeared as human as Leoten, or so they seemed under all the armor and concealing garb.

He looks around the room he'd taken shelter in. It was some kind of experimental lab, where magi and scientists could work together. No doubt, they used places like this to develop new dragons and other creations here within Idraster Base.

Leoten moved between different pieces of lab equipment, tables, and stools. Most of the center of the room was taken up by a single large, circular tank of water that went to the ceiling and descended through the floor. The liquid within appeared misty at first as if the inside was full of some kind of floating debris. He approached close to the tank, then circled it cautiously, knife in hand. He kept his eyes on the water.

A ripple appeared inside the tank and a mind flew toward him through the water. Leoten retreated in apprehension. The shadow of a creature twice his height loomed in the tank. It was not humanoid, but neither was it totally fish-like. The creature looked like a huge eel with elongated human arms. A lamprey-like mouth and large eyes on the front of its body drifted just a few feet just to over the arms. The creature was long but built thick with muscle and the long tail trailed off into the dim water where Leoten couldn't see. One wide, human hand pressed to the side of the tank.

Leoten stared at the bizarre creature, completely unfamiliar with it. It was clearly no dragon and no shoddok. *How many creatures had been crafted in this place? How many other oddities awaited here?* He didn't dare guess.

Leoten paced around the tank but the creature followed him wherever he went in the room. Its eyes glowed yellow like those of a great cat. Peering out of the tank at him, watching him with keen and curious intelligence.

He wanted to say something, but couldn't think of any way to communicate with the creature except by touch with his mind-eater abilities. He didn't dare risk any more trouble than he had already. His mission was to get Nerida out of this base.

How was he going to reach her before those mercenaries did? He looked for another exit to the room and found one, but he didn't like it.

The grate on the floor looked to be some kind of water drain at first, but he spotted the shadow of a ladder within, possibly for maintenance on the drainage channel. He lifted the metal grill and climbed through the narrow gap. The creature in the room above him peered as he descended. A kind of whine issued from the tank and then the large tail thumped against the transparent wall. Leoten paused, halfway into the pipe and motioned with his arms in an attempt to calm the creature. The barrier held and the eel-man slipped away from into the mist.

Leoten descended the ladder to a lower level, and then crept along a low and narrow passageway where the heating piles that kept the the main floors warm made him sweat in his seal suit. He quickly found another grate large enough for him to crawl through on the wall.

He crawled from the tight space with of the maintenance passage and emerged into another room full of lab equipment. Electrical plant piles buzzed with different interface screens and other attachments pressed into them to access their memory. Plant piles could be used to store information, as well as produce energy to fuel machines. They provided most of humanity's technology in the eastern parts of the continent. Though animal piles were common here in the Dragon Lands, they were rare everywhere else, and plant piles remained in heavy use in the gardens of the western coast.

Otrusia grew plenty of them as well, despite the latitude it seemed.

Leoten moved silently among the piles. He made no sound, but his equipment and limbs moved with heaviness as more pain began to creep along them from the impact of Hargruss hurling him into the wall on the first level.

He turned a corner and found a security door at the end of the pile room. He'd found no other humans inside, and no other odd creatures either. He peered through the passage beyond, but found it empty.

Either the Otrusian guards must been scrambled from this level as well or the enemy had already devastated them as well. He returned to the pile room where the sun lamp no doubt used to keep the plants alive to flickered on. Those lamps would be necessary because the room would get little, if any natural light at least thirty feet below the surface.

He went to one of the terminals connected to a plant pile. He tapped the screen and found it accessible. He began to read some of the memories compiled there.

The pile's information on the experiments seemed spotty, but Leoten was no science-magus. He accessed most of it without pass-codes to specific sections of the files with the plant structure. However, the protections of the higher security portions would take far too long for him to crack on his own. If the mercenaries captured the base they might be able to get more information about the project from this room.

He quickly skimmed the the schematic of the base, the one that was easily accessible at the at the top of the file structure. He grimaced to himself with a slight satisfaction that he found the base had six levels, though the lowest one looked to be for maintenance only. He was on the second submerged floor, just one below the top. Idraster went all the way to the ocean floor at the central support column of the base. Every floor was used for different kinds of experiments.

Leoten couldn't tell exactly what test were conducted on each level, but he noted at least one lab on every floor. *Damn it,* he thought. *This is too large a place for one agent to handle.*

He looked up from the terminal, and kept his eyes on the door as he removed one of the sets of communication fungus and thimbles from the mission case. He put the sprout in his ear, and then used them the thimble with a microphone to connect himself to Damaia back on the cruiser. His supervisor answered him with the weary sound of a yawn.

"Damaia," he said. "Listen. It's Red."

"Red," said Damaia. "It's been too long since you went in there. It's past 8 now."

"I understand," said Leoten. "I haven't been able to get close to Nerida yet."

"We heard, we detected some odd traffic around the base," said Damaia. "Two small boats arrived, the second ten minutes after the first."

"Yeah," said Leoten. "Looks like they the first of those boats carried some kind of invader."

"Invaders?" asked Damaia "Another attacker at the base?"

"Seems that way," said Leoten. "And they brought a powerful magus, a sorcerer or something greater, with them." He relayed what he'd seen of Hargruss. "I don't know if I can stop that beast by myself."

"Well I don't know about you but there is more bad news," said Damaia. "The second landing boat appears to belong to Drufan."

"A Drufanesh landing team?" said Leoten. "How do you know?"

"We recognized their transmission from intercepted communications, though we couldn't break thte code." Damaia sighed. "It seems you're not going to be alone in this mission, Red."

"Do you think they sent more of their elite agents?" said Leoten.

"I can't say for sure on that," said Damaia. "The first boat could have had enough of a team on board they might be able to capture the entire base."

"And now, with the sorcerer on the base," said Leoten. "He's far too dangerous for any attackers."

"Telekinetic powers," said Damaia. "That doesn't sound like anything we've encountered before. I never even heard of it except among the gods and goddesses who could sometimes have abilities like that."

"He's no god," said Leoten. "I made him bleed already. But I don't know if I can kill them."

"Don't worry about him," said Damaia. "Get Nerida out of that place. Get out of there and leave the rest to Drufan if you must. Let the others fight it out."

"I'll do what I can," said Leoten.

"I think I hear a protest in your tone." Damaia clicked her tongue. "Don't do it, Red. You have to keep the mission firmly in mind. You have to do everything you can to accomplish our goal because we need an Iron Dragon in the TCR and we need the help of people who know how to make them."

"I understand," said Leoten. "But you're right. I don't want to see this base taken over by Drufan."

"Focus on the mission," said Damaia. "You went into that place to save Nerida, not anyone else. You're not a hero. You're an agent for the Triumvirate of Custodial Republics. Think of our honor and the mission will follow."

"I know." Leoten broke the connection with the fungal pile by removing his thimble-clad fingertip from his ear. *Damaia can talk all she wants about the Republics and their honor.* Nationalism didn't present as a reason for action to Leoten. He took the sprout out of his ear and put it back in the container, then replaced the whole kit in the mission case.

He carefully removed his service pistol and attached the silencer. If matters got any uglier than they already were, nothing might be able to stop the escalation. He had no idea where it would end if things progressed much more.

Hargruss cut straight through his agency's entire plan and left it in shambles.

Who is that monster?

He started into the passage, moving as stealthily as he could.

• • • •

CHAPTER 5

Leoten made his way down the passage and into another chamber, through a hatchway. The room on the other side stank of fish, as if a fresh catch was moldering somewhere nearby. Yet, it appeared to be another laboratory based on the furnishings. Steel tables covered in beakers and vials stood unattended all around the room. Chalk drawings on the surfaces of a massive wood-paneled blackboard covered one wall opposite the hatch door.

The drawings didn't resemble anything living, or even geometric shapes similar to those used in medical rituals. Of course, magi and scientists were the same when it came to experiments. Both required written materials in both followed similar processes. He looked around the room and noticed a slight figure cringing behind one of the tables. Her knees knocked together.

He crept into the room, knowing that she'd already seen him. Whoever she was, she must not be trained to defend the base. He held his pistol with the barrel pointed downward and approached the table quietly. She trembled but didn't reveal that she'd noticed him.

He held back from getting too close. She might be frightened into reckless action if he attempted to approach her openly. She could be another magus, or possibly one of their lab assistants.

He gazed down the barrel of his weapon. Then lowered the gun and kept his eyes steady. She looked up and met his gaze as he rounded the side of the table. Her dark hair, black as night, and pale somewhat southerly skin made him guess she didn't come from Otrusia. The people here tended toward the more toward quite a different appearance, given the latitude and their adaptations to less sunlight.

"Who are you?" she asked.

"Call me Red," he said. "Who are you?"

"Red? You must be the infiltrator security told us about." Her eyes narrowed. She put one hand on the tabletop beside her. "What kind of mission are you on?"

"I'm here to retrieve magi from the lab who are being held against their will."

"Really?" She shuddered and ducked back behind the table. "That would describe me, but I don't think you mean to take me out of here."

"That depends," said Leoten. "If I can get anybody out at all, I'm taking as many people as I can. The space is compromised. Another operations team has attacked already."

"You sound Volskan," said Maia.

"I'm from Volskorod," he said. "And that's where I'm going back to when I'm done."

"You won't get far without a plan to escape through the cold water."

"Leave that to me," he said.

"Too much to explain." She nodded. "I get it."

"Do you have any idea what this room is for?" asked Leoten. "What is the symbol on the wall?"

"It's a bonding sigil." She looked at Leoten with furtive eyes as she smoothed out the black trousers that she wore under her lab coat. "You see. "I helped the project. I helped make some of the hybrid creatures we created in this base."

"Hybrids?" said Leoten. "Is that what Idraster base is for?"

"Yes." The woman lowered her eyes from his face. "My name is Maia. I've been working with the other magi here."

"Maia," said Leoten. "Do you have any idea where they'd take Nerida in an emergency like this?"

"You're looking for Nerida?" said Maia. "That makes sense."

"Do you know where she is?" asked Leoten.

"I think so," she said. "But there are two other magi here who are here against their will. We need to get Volo and Hayin out as well."

"Volo and Hayin," said Leoten. "We'll see if we can find them."

"What kind of attackers are in this other team?" asked Maia.

"You were down here than when the invaders struck?" said Leoten. "I'm not sure exactly who they are. Their leader, though—I think he's some kind of monster. His name is Hargruss. I don't know if we can stop him in a direct fight. No magic I used worked, and I doubt anything an ordinary magus could do would accomplish much more, based on what I've seen."

His teeth went on edge.

"Hargruss," she said. "That name is unfamiliar. It doesn't even sound like it belongs to Drufan or anywhere else I know."

"Agreed," said Leoten. "Now, stay close to me. We need to get moving and find Nerida and the other magi."

The two of them went to a door that Maia indicated led closer to the emergency chamber on the second level where the chief might take Nerida in the event of an emergency.

She leaned closer to check the locks. "It's a security room."

"Good," said Leoten. "Hopefully they'll all be there."

Maia nodded. Her round eyes were wide with fear. She looked back at the room where they that they just left, then darted away from the door by a few paces.

"What are you doing?" asked Leoten.

"I forgot." Maia's face flushed. "I need to bring one of the samples with us."

"Fine," said Leoten. "But be quick about it." He covered her with his pistol trained on the far door where he'd come into the lab. Then he glanced over his shoulder to check and make certain that the direction they were going didn't provide any further surprises.

She returned with a box tucked under her arm. "This isn't really just a sample. It's a whole specimen. We created it here."

"Could be valuable," said Leoten. "Keep it safe."

"No problem there," said Maia.

The two of them went into the room beyond the main laboratory, where another set of laboratory tables and more experiments surrounded a magical sigil drawn on one wall. The room was empty of people but the reinforced door in the far wall was secured by locks and latches that looked stronger than the other hatchways.

"That's the security room," said Maia.

"We need to find a way inside," said Leoten.

"I know how," she said. "But it's going to hurt me."

"What do you mean?" asked Leoten.

"I'm a blood magus," said Maia. "It won't require much force if I can use my magic to get the door open."

"Go ahead then," said Leoten. "I'll watch your back."

Maia produced a small pin from a pocket box on her belt and pricked herself with it. The blood on her fingertip began to flow and then formed into the shape of a key that easily fit into the door's heaviest lock. When she was done with that, she changed the key to a different shape, then unlocked a different latch. She continued this process for a few minutes until the door swung inward.

"That should do it." She replaced the pin in the box. "Is anyone back there?"

Leoten peered into the chamber of the security room and found just a hint of what he'd been looking for. Nerida had left her white coat there with a few long red hairs stretched upon it.

He grimaced. "We're too late, whoever's attacking the base made in here first."

"Or the enemy forced them to leave somehow." Maia's hands trembled. "Crane is quick to move his 'assets' to safety."

"The station chief?" said Leoten. "He could be trying to evacuate them somewhere else."

"There is an underwater locust dock on the third level," said Maia. "The chief might try to take the others there."

"We need to get further below," said Leoten. "Are there any other places Crane and the other magi could've gone?"

"I don't think so." Maia frowned. "These attackers sound too dangerous for security to push them back to the surface."

"One of them is," Leoten said. "Lead the way, Maia."

• • • •

CHAPTER 6

The cargo lift carried them to a locust dock on the third level beneath the surface. The doors slid open and then locked into place on either side of the car.

Leoten held out a hand to stop Maia from leaving the elevator. She glanced at him, then froze as she saw the situation before them. He pointed to the cluster of people by the pool of water where the locust floated below them and she nodded. He took the lead as they crept onto the upper walkway that led over the pool where the locust waited under the surface.

He glimpsed a shock of red hair among them. Nerida stood in her black blouse and trousers, flanked by two other magi, a man and a woman, the ones he'd seen her alongside in the mess hall. The station chief stood over the pool. Blood trickled from a freshly dressed wound on his right shoulder and a pistol hung loosely in his fingers below that.

"We're lucky this supply beast arrived today," he said. "It'll be just a few moments before she surfaces."

As the locust's sleek, manta shape surfaced little by little, the elevator doors slid shut with a hum. Maia glanced at Leoten. The station chief cursed under his breath.

"Someone must have hit the call button. That monster won't be long now."

Maia inhaled sharply.

Leoten turned to her and shook his head. He trained his pistol on the station chief. "Give them up, Crane," he called. "You can't out shoot me from down there."

"Red." The station chief growled low in his throat. "Damn it, you Triumvirate fools don't die easily."

Nerida spun and her eyes widened. Leoten met her gaze but kept Crane at gunpoint. "Sorry for my poor timing," he said. "Nerida."

The station chief's pistol twitched to point at the flame magus.

"You're not too late. Not yet," she said. Nerida's gaze shifted to Crane. "John."

The chief's hand trembled.

"Crane, put down the gun," said Leoten. "Don't do anything stupid just because you're desperate."

The elevator doors hummed as they began to open again.

"Damn you all!" Crane's finger moved within the trigger guard of his pistol.

Leoten shot the station chief twice in the chest. John Crane spasmed and he dropped his pistol. The station chief's body toppled into the pool of icy water, even as the locust fully reached the surface.

"Are you three alright?" Leoten called to Nerida.

"I think so," she said. "Volo, Hayin?"

"I'm fine," said the gray-haired man.

The slender, dark-haired woman nodded. "No worse than before."

Maia glanced over her shoulder at the elevator. An elongated, skeletal shadow fell onto the floor below the walkway, cast by a flare of light from within the car.

"It's Hargruss," said Leoten. "We need to board that locust. Can any of you control it?"

"We'll figure that out later." Nerida took Volo and Hayin by the arms and climbed the short ramp to the top of the pool. The muscular hatch on the side of the locust opened with a sickly sound. Leoten turned his pistol on Hargruss as Maia began to climb down the ladder from the walkway to reach the locust.

The demonic sorcerer moved languidly, completely unconcerned with Leoten or his weapon. His rictus mouth grinned impossibly wide. "You travel fast," said the sorcerer, but not fast enough. You are the same as you were when I first sensed you in Fyon."

Blood flooded Leoten's face and adrenaline coursed in his mind. He made himself lower the barrel of his gun. He couldn't risk giving Hargruss projectiles to deflect, in case he hurt the magi. A kind of placidity replaced his anger at the demon's taunts.

"What are you after, Hargruss?"

"Do you ever stop asking questions, Red?"

Leoten flared his mental defenses as a cold presence, one he remembered from the hotel in Fyon months ago, touched his thoughts. His barriers crumbled at Hargruss's mere caress, but before the foreign presence could enter Leoten's mind proper, a peaceful strength bloomed within him, a kind of confidence that refused to give up, and not out of mere defiance, but filled with resolve.

He shoved Hargruss's attack from his mind as the hatch at the locust's boarding bridge lowered, allowing the magi the chance to board.

Another presence resolved itself within the locust's passenger hold as Nerida and Hayin stepped onto the bridge, red and black side by side. Leoten's eyes narrowed as he focused on Hargruss's white figure.

"Don't try to follow us out of here," he told the sorcerer.

"That beast won't take you from this place." Hargruss drew back his hand, palm flat, as if ready to deliver a slap to the empty air over the pool. Leoten aimed his pistol and fired twice at the pallid, bony figure.

Hargruss' wide mouth contracted in a snarl. One bullet clipped his collar and the other went through his raised hand. Scarlet spots flecked across skeletal fingers and palm. The sorcerer spun and swatted at Leoten. A rush of force hurled him from the walkway and into open air over the floor of the dock three meters below.

He skidded on the iron floor, but somehow managed to land upright despite the force of the impact, and kept his grip on the gun. Leoten had no time to check for injuries. He raced under the walkway and toward the boarding bridge. Maia descended to regroup with the others on the ramp at the bottom of the ladder.

Leoten slowed to a stumble on his way up the ramp toward the locust.

Hargruss steadily descended the stairs from the elevator. The sorcerer's unhurried pace betrayed a deep-seated arrogance and infuriated Leoten. Hargruss reached for the hilt of the sword that extended over his shoulder. Leoten called his signature knife, ready to hold off the enemy as long as he could to let the locust escape.

A pair of cowled and heavily-armored mercenaries scurried to the top of the stairs behind Hargruss, automatic rifles in their hands. Leoten grimaced and looked over his shoulder only to find all four magi standing as if paralyzed outside the locust.

"It seems not all of you can resist my abilities," said Hargruss.

From inside the hollow of the locust, there came the sound of footsteps.

Leoten met Hargruss's grotesque eyes. Unlike the sorcerer, Leoten's powers required a medium, usually touch to affect their subjects. Hargruss might not be able to maintain any more magic than what he'd used to keep the magi from boarding the locust, but he might not need to if he could use the sword he drew from the sheathe on his back.

The weapon glistened like quicksilver and the blade grew as Leoten watched. What had seemed a wide short sword quickly became a longer, more slender weapon of the same material, though it held the same curved edge. Leoten held his dagger in a defensive position, unsure if his blade could manage a fatal blow on Hargruss even if he found a chance to strike.

The calm he'd experienced when he resisted Hargruss's mind magic began to subside. In the wake of that emotion remained grim determination.

"Leoten," a woman's voice said from behind him. "You can't win this alone."

He gritted his teeth. "I have to try, Nerida."

The sound of footsteps behind him stopped on the bridge. Maia gasped and then all four magi behind Leoten collapsed slowly to the floor. He whirled toward the source of the steps as they fell.

A woman dressed in layered clothes over a gray seal wetsuit stood on the boarding bridge of the locust. Her dark hair drifted short of shoulder-length and her eyes held ferocity and compassion in equal measure.

"Aunwe? What are you doing here?" Leoten asked.

She shook her head. "No time for that. We need to get these four aboard."

Hargruss bellowed a laugh which made Leoten spin to face the demon. As he turned, Hargruss swung his sword the force of his kinetic palm focused in a tighter strike. Aunwe cringed to the floor but the locust behind her shrieked in pain from the magical blow.

The locust thrashed and hurled Aunwe into the pool. The muscular hatch on the beast's side sealed and it dived into the icy pool. The motion kicked up freezing salt foam that splashed all the way to the ceiling of the dock. Leoten's heart sank, as their chance of escape vanished in the spray of blood and seawater.

• • • •

CHAPTER 7

Hargruss howled like a jungle ape. He tossed his head from side to side as he advanced on Leoten and the cluster of subdued magi beside the pool.

Nerida stirred, but her eyes couldn't seem to focus, so using her flames would be out of the question. Leoten couldn't think of her, or worry if Aunwe was alright. The sorcerer before him demanded his full attention.

He lunged at Hargruss, signature knife ready to slash. The skinny, hairless arms of the pale demon formed a v-shape as he gripped the hilt of his elongated sword in both hands.

Hargruss parried Leoten's first strike. The reverse movement cut a gash across the white demon's forearm. Hargruss didn't flinch.

The shape-shifting sword swept in a wide arc toward Leoten's midsection. He barely moved out of reach in time to avoid the blow. With lazy casualness, the sorcerer reversed the blade and cut back the way he'd swung.

Leoten ducked as he retreated past the magi on the floor. His heel hit the slope at the pool's side.

The vile grin on Hargruss' face appeared frozen and static as he stopped and slung the fallen form of Maia over his arm. The sorcerer turned to grab Nerida as the flame magus rolled onto her back. She groaned and tried to push his hand away with her arms. He seized the collar of her dark blouse and jerked her off the floor with ease.

Leoten flipped his signature knife through the air as Hargruss straightened his back. The blade clipped across the bald, demonic scalp. The blood that flicked forth looked pink as a sunrise, illuminated by the glow piles in the ceiling. Hargruss shifted his free hand and touched the wound. The cut sealed under his thumb with a hiss of steam.

The sorcerer shook his head as Leoten recalled the signature knife to his hand.

"As entertaining as you are to play with, Leoten, I think your time is up." He turned his back on Leoten, Nerida over one shoulder and the unconscious Maia on his other arm. "I have other games to attend to now."

Hargruss marched away, carrying the two women without apparent effort. Leoten raised his knife to throw, but the aggression he sensed in the mercenaries on the walkway before him made him pause. He couldn't avoid multiple rifle shots if they opened fire, and neither Hayin nor Volo would survive the barrage. He ground his teeth as he lowered the blade and backed toward the pool.

Hargruss's soldiers didn't open fire but held their guns trained on Leoten. The sorcerer climbed the metal stairs to the elevator car. He disappeared inside the car and the soldiers backed in after him. The doors closed. Leoten cursed.

The magi left beside him were unconscious but unhurt. Leoten climbed the ramp to the pool to look for Aunwe. He offered a silent prayer that she'd not been hit by Hargruss's telekinetic strike.

Leoten scanned the pool water with its spiraling traces of red locust blood. He found no sign of Aunwe. *Was she pulled out of the dock in the beast's wake? Could she have gone under and beeen lost in the icy freeze beyond the water lock?* But as he looked and the flakes of debris and swirls of bubbles faded, a warm presence reached out to him from close by.

He thrust one hand over the water and Aunwe's elegant glove clasped his dry-suited wrist. She'd been clinging to the side of the pool. He helped her over the side and for a moment, her hands found his shoulders and gripped tight.

"Thank you."

He looked into her eyes. "Drufan sent you, didn't they?"

She squeezed her eyes shut and took a deep breath before she opened them again. "In one matter of speaking, yes. Otherwise, no."

"Save the details, Aunwe. We need to get these two moving and find the others."

She shivered, then released his shoulders. "I understand. That monster drove off the locust I'd commandeered, so we'll need another means of extraction. Have you got communication to a team off-base?"

He rolled the thimble he used to connect to the fungal network onto his thumb, then nodded. "Have you?"

"I have some members outside." She knelt beside Hayin. "Are you alright, Hay?"

The woman stirred, raising her head. "That could have gone more to plan."

"She's one of yours?" asked Leoten.

Aunwe helped Hayin stand. "She is."

"But he isn't?" Leoten motioned to Volo's unconscious form.

"He's one of our VIPs for extraction," said Aunwe, "along with Nerida and Maia. After that mess in Volskorod late last year I convinced my agency in the DGD to take dragon-building more seriously."

Leoten folded his arms. He guessed Aunwe might be using the DGD as much as they thought they were using her. "I get it." He showed her a small smile. "Can you work with me for now?"

"For now, I think." Aunwe frowned. "The nature of the mission won't change, but Hay." She turned to Hayin. "I wasn't able to hear the end of your last connection."

The magus-scientist tugged at the long bun of her hair. "I tried to warn you he wasn't an ordinary magus, or warrior."

"I see that now." Aunwe glanced at Leoten. "Have you got any intelligence on him?"

"I only know his name and what I've witnessed," he said. "He's called Hargruss and he's some kind of mind sorcerer beyond being an elemental magus."

"He's stronger than you, isn't he?" said Aunwe.

"You could tell?"

"I guessed."

"He can project his mental attacks, so either he's learned a kind of mind magic I don't understand, or—"

Aunwe snapped her fingers. "He could have a spirit adept working with him."

Leoten's brows bent inward and he nodded. "He could."

"Hayin," said Aunwe. "You need to take Volo and look for another way to the surface. The magus agent wiped the traces of tears from her eyes. Aunwe frowned. "Why were you crying?"

"I don't get it either," said Hayin. "I only remember a voice in my head, and then I was on the floor."

"It's possible Hargruss's powers have hormonal side effects," said Leoten. "Some mind-eaters are rougher when they make contact than others."

"I remember," said Aunwe.

"All I remember is static." Hayin arched a refined brow. She knelt to wake up Volo.

• • • •

THE DEMON SAID THAT in his eyes, the edges of objects appeared to fray into shadows, while people blazed like open flames. Hargruss moved without effort, despite carrying two women over his shoulders. He didn't make any gesture to ask Joachim or his men to help with his captives.

Joachim Zodai had learned many things from the demon called Hargruss in the past few months. First and foremost of his lessons was never to ask questions of his bizarre employer. Second...

They entered a laboratory on the second level of the base. Hargruss stood before the cloudy tank of water in the center of the room and peered into the depths.

"Someone's in there," said the demon.

The other two mercenaries Joachim had brought with them exchanged glances. The quickness of their eyes betrayed their fear. They knew as well as he not to ask questions. If they ever planned to see the surface again Hargruss needed to get what he wanted.

The demon took a deep breath through his wide, lipless mouth.

"Zodai, take your men and, leave us now." Hargruss tugged the unconscious body of the black-haired Maia with one hand and positioned her along his arm as if she weighed nothing. "Stand guard outside. I must conduct the ritual to reforge my bond with the Touchwork."

"What are you going to do with her?" asked one of the men, a veteran of the Letheri Campaign where he'd fought the Bruise Regiment under Joachim's command.

"Who asks?" Hargruss's voice sounded like a cracking eggshell.

"I'm Corporal Thenno Kalvis." He thrust out his chin. "I've been with you since you started to work with the Zodai Company."

"I know you, child." Hargruss turned his head just a few degrees and the edge of his maw showed around the curve of his head.

"Apologies for him, Hargruss." Joachim bowed before the white demon. "He meant nothing by it."

"I know."

"Of course you do."

"Leave us, Zodai. Replace Corporal Kalvis on my guard detail."

"At once, sir." Joachim glared at Kalvis, then took his fellow mercenary by the arm and tugged him toward the hatchway. The private on guard followed them to the door. "Warriors needn't question gods."

The corporal hung his head as they went. Once they cleared the hatch, though, he was the one to move to close the way behind them.

"Most wise," said Hargruss in a sharp voice that carried across the lab. "Perhaps there is hope for you, yet, Corporal Kalvis."

Kalvis trembled, then sealed the hatch shut. Joachim kept his mouth shut.

• • • •

CHAPTER 8

Aunwe's warmth of spirit spread from her unrequested but welcome, comforting Leoten's rattled senses. More peace welled up from the dragon within him in response to her presence. He hadn't been aware of how much better he'd connected with the dragon before their reunion.

She removed her sodden outer layers of clothes to reveal a form-fitting, dark-colored seal suit underneath. Her eyes found his as she wrapped a pale scarf around her neck.

"Do you know any way out of here other than the elevator?" She arched a brow.

The flush that had arisen in his face a moment ago felt cold in the next instant. "No," he said. "But there must be a way."

Hayin put an arm around Volo's shoulders. "It's alright," she said. "We can make you a path to catch up with them."

"You're both blood magi, right?" said Leoten.

Hayin nodded. "How about we help these two, Volo?"

The male magus nodded, face pale and scrunched like he was about to be sick. "I'll try."

"I can take the lead on the incantation and offering. All you need to do is support."

"I can handle that," he said.

Hayin glanced toward Aunwe. "You and Red should be ready to fight before you leave. We don't know what things are like upstairs."

Aunwe turned over her palm and winced at the burn of her weapon bond's activation. The machine pistol that appeared in her grip was familiar to Leoten, and moved lightly, empty of rounds, as almost all firearms arrived when called to hand by magic.

He reloaded his sidearm, then produced his signature knife from the bond on his hand. Aunwe met his gaze again. "Ready?"

"As I can be. What kind of spell are you going to work, Hayin?"

The slim magus frowned as she produced a tiny vial of blood from a travel case. "The four of us mixed our blood in here in case we got separated. Our magic can't transport you straight to the but with the correct incantation we can guide you there."

"If we have to use the elevator we're sitting targets," said Aunwe.

"I know." Hayin grimaced. "But I don't think there's a faster way up there."

A wave of calm crested in the back of Leoten's mind, bringing with it a message from the dragon's ghost, like the spray of a salt sea.

"The elevator will work," he said, suddenly confident. "But we can't use that blood to locate them if this is going to work."

Both women looked at him with curiosity.

"Sounds like you have a plan," said Volo, still supporting himself gingerly against Hayin's shoulder.

"Not exactly," Leoten said. "But those mercenaries are the main obstacle right now. If we can get by them, we can catch Hargruss and save Maia and Nerida."

"Sorry, but there's no blood magic that can knock out a dozen soldiers from here," said Hayin. "Unless you know something I don't about blood magic."

"I know nothing about it," said Leoten. "But the dragon I'm keeping close does. There's power in all types of blood, and the dragon suggested we can use it to disguise ourselves."

"I don't know any shifting incantations," said Hayin.

"Sounds as though we may not need such things," said Volo. "Tell us the details, Red. Be quick."

Leoten took a deep breath, and then, guided by the dragon's thoughts, explained the plan.

· · · ·

JOACHIM GRUNTED AS the hatchway leading to the elevator's service station flipped open before him. A pair of his troopers in full masks, who'd been on guard to keep the enemy agents from pursuit marched through, carrying the thin, dark-haired magus woman Hargruss had left behind between them. She appeared to still be unconscious and her shoes dragged on the floor. A trickle of blood dripped from each palm and her head dangled limp on her shoulders.

"What happened?" asked Joachim.

The bigger trooper shook his head. "Can't believe she'd try it," he said. "She came upstairs looking to help her friends."

"I didn't hear any shots." Joachim's eyes narrowed. "How did she get like this?"

Corporal Kalvis and the other man on watch with Joachim stepped forward, but he waved them back. "Hold. I want to inspect her, personally. Can't be too careful with a magus."

The shorter of the two soldiers grunted as she maneuvered the unconscious magus onto a bench along the wall. "Before we took her down, she said she knew where Hargruss was."

"What about the TCR agent, that man called Red?"

"We didn't see him," said the female soldier, whose name Joachim couldn't quite recall with her face hidden. "But we should warn the boss."

"Kalvis," said Joachim. Watch these three. I'm going to meet with him. I'll do it alone. No sense in risking all of us."

"Thank you, sir."

Joachim Zodai ground his teeth together. "Don't mention it. Far as I can tell, the greatest danger to us left on this base is on our side." He opened the hatchway opposite the one the others had brought the magus through. With reluctant steps, he marched toward the laboratory doors.

• • • •

LEOTEN WATCHED THE mercenary leader reach for the door to the lab with the tank of cloudy water inside it. He glanced at Aunwe. She still wore the magical disguise Hayin and Volo had created for her from their blood magic. They'd done the same for Leoten to allow them to get past the elevator guards.

"What now?" he asked.

"What do you think?" she whispered in reply.

"I think we don't have time." He grimaced. "We need to move."

"Agreed." She put a hand on his wrist, then slipped her fingers gently under the material at the end of his sleeve. Skin-to-skin contact might improve the connection of their abilities. Either way, her touch exhilarated him. Together they lashed out at the mercenaries in the room with them, draining them of their wakefulness in quick succession.

Hayin opened her eyes. "We're close, aren't we?" she said.

"Yes. Follow me and prepare to fight." Aunwe's fingers slipped from Leoten's arm. She ran after the mercenary leader as the hatch opened at the end of the passage. Leoten drew his pistol and followed her, with Hayin close behind him.

As they charged, Leoten drew his signature knife from its hot, tattooed bond. As the mercenary leader reached for the handle of the hatchway, Leoten released his weapon. The blade stabbed into the mercenary's hand, then reappeared in Leoten's grasp a moment later.

The man turned slowly, eyes widening. "What are you—?"

Leoten slammed into the mercenary and pinned him against the hatch. The man's head hit the frame and he collapsed. Leoten took a deep breath. "Now or never."

Aunwe inhaled sharply, but nodded to him, indicating she was ready for the fight.

He pushed the unconscious mercenary leader out of the way and then hauled the hatch open.

• • • •

CHAPTER 9

A red glow came from within the chamber beyond the hatch. Leoten stepped inside, signature knife in a guard position. Hargruss' lanky figure knelt over the unconscious women before the tank of cloudy water. Amid a crimson tint, Leoten glimpsed Nerida's sweat-streaked face where she lay on the floor beside Maia's limp legs. The red light issued from gill-like openings in the demonic sorcerer's flesh as he loomed above the two of them. The openings flared on his neck and back but his face remained turned from the hatch door.

Aunwe gritted her teeth and took aim with her pistol.

"He has to know we're here," said Leoten. "Be careful."

She lowered the barrel of her weapon and turned to Hayin. The blood magus nodded. She drew back her sleeve to reveal a series of pale horizontal scars on her forearm and held out her palm toward Hargruss, ready to counter the sorcerer's magic.

Leoten crept between laboratory desks. His vision narrowed on Hargruss' back. Maia groaned and her eyelids fluttered. Hargruss waved his hand over her face and her eyes closed again as the demon extracted her will to awaken. Leoten reached Hargruss and readied his blade to plunge into his enemy's neck.

"You won't do that," said Hargruss in a low voice. "The Corporeum won't lose two agents in this world the same way so soon."

The memory of a woman bleeding to death in Leoten's arms returned along with those words. His eyes widened in disbelief. The corner of Hargruss's bizarrely wide mouth turned slightly into view.

"You remember Jennika. She might have lived if she'd kept on guard."

Leoten's lip twitched with rage and he brought his knife down. Hargruss ignored him, still on his knees. The metal of his shapeshifting sword flowed from the scabbard and deflected Leoten's blade from the demon's neck.

"I'm surprised you'd try that, knowing how futile it would be." Hargruss grinned. "Why keep fighting, Red?"

Leoten recoiled, knife shaking in his grip. Behind him, Aunwe sent her spirit to shield Leoten's mind just as Hargruss' magic struck at him. She tussled with the demon's mind, then hurled the power of the sorcerer back to its source.

Hargruss stood and whirled in the same motion. "You dare?" he hissed. "You're bold for a wielder of spirit. Perhaps I shouldn't have dismissed you so swiftly."

Aunwe and Hayin followed Leoten's path to get a few steps closer to Hargruss and his captives. The pale demon didn't draw his blade but flexed the bony fingers on both hands. Leoten stabbed at him, but Hargruss swept out with his palm and sent him staggering back with an invisible gale-force wind, that nonetheless carried less power than before, thanks to Hayin's drain on his powers. His leg and hip hit the supports of one lab table with a crack. He grunted in pain.

"Red!" Aunwe cried.

"You've got more immediate worries than him," said a man from the hatchway. A steel knife glinted in each of the mercenary leader's hands. He shoved Hayin to the floor as he rushed at Aunwe. The blood magus fell prone and Hargruss' impossible grin widened as the mystic suppression she'd activated faded to nothing. He swept out his hand and the wind hurled Leoten across the room. He tumbled past Hayin and landed on his agonized back on the metal floor.

Dazed, Leoten rolled onto his side. He flipped his dagger to throw at the mercenary leader as Aunwe dodged away from a flurry of knife blows from the man's blades. The mercenary grinned. "You can't avoid the blade forever, woman."

She said nothing, but her leg lashed out with a kick to her opponent's knee. The mercenary staggered. A second kick made him retreat a meter, but not fast enough to avoid the third. The man's knee cracked and his leg went out from under him. The mercenary leader collapsed against the wall, but even as he fell he flipped his dagger to throwing position.

Leoten hurled his signature knife at the mercenary's wrist. A bellow from Hargruss and a rush of telekinetic wind blew the weapon off course and through the open hatchway beside its mark. The leader's dagger flew into Aunwe's collar. Blood began to well up from the wound it tore through her coat. The blade tumbled away across a lab table. Aunwe cried out and lurched against the table behind her.

Leoten returned his signature knife to his grip. The bond seal burned on his hand. The mercenary leader ducked and limped through the hatchway to seek cover behind the frame.

"Fox!" Hayin got to her feet. "How bad is it?"

"It won't stop me." Aunwe grimaced.

Leoten rushed Hargruss cut high and then quickly struck again, but low this time. He opened two wounds on the demonic sorcerer's forearms, but his opponent kept the blade from his neck and head.

"Stop these struggles, they are useless," said Hargruss.

"The hell they are." Aunwe raised her machine pistol and released a volley at him. Three rounds struck Hargruss in the chest and another cut through the corner of his mouth. He staggered backward. One overlong arm dragged along the floor and found Maia as she stirred. His fingers closed around her collar and hauled her up to put her body between him and Aunwe.

Aunwe cursed as she returned her pistol, all ammunition spent, to the shrine where it rested when not in use. Leoten slipped around Hargruss and Maia and stabbed his signature knife into the demon's hip. Pinkish blood issued around the blade and Hargruss sank to one knee as the leg below gave out.

"Captain Zodai, your team has failed." Hargruss' grin never faltered. He swung out with Maia. Her legs and side crashed into Leoten's back. Both of them slammed into the side of the clouded tank with a crunch that cracked the reinforced glass. Leoten coughed a trickle of blood and closed his eyes in agony.

Hargruss reached for Nerida where she lay, but the red-haired magus was gone. Hargruss looked around, his eyes wild. "Where did you go?" He fixed his gaze upon Aunwe and Hayin. "Enough of this!" He drew the sword from his back. Aunwe rolled under one of the lab tables while Hayin hurtled in the opposite direction. Leoten pushed himself up on his knees as fine streams of misty water began to flow from the cracked side of the tank.

The demon thrust out his blade and the weapon elongated to cross the room like a straight quicksilver bolt of electricity. Hayin waved her palm to ward off aggressive magic, but the silver sword flowed forth as if she'd done nothing. The point slashed past Hayin's neck and she fell to the floor out of sight, trailing a streak of blood.

"Hayin!" Aunwe called, but the blood magus didn't answer.

Hargruss looked both directions as the blade of his sword roiled and withdrew to its ordinary length.

Leoten lunged at Hargruss's legs and tackled the sorcerer to the floor. His foe's sword flew from his hand. Leoten raised the signature knife to strike.

Hargruss snarled and lashed out to shove against Leoten's wrist and hold back the blade. They struggled for a moment, but Hargruss' wounded arms quickly began to lose the fight with Leoten's body weight. The tip of the knife sank toward the sorcerer's chest.

"Do you think that will kill me?" hissed the demonic mouth.

Leoten grunted. "You do." His voice sounded harsh and his breath appeared like steam.

"Even if you best me," Hargruss said, "you won't escape this place."

Leoten's knife cut slowly into Hargruss' pale flesh above the heart, but the wound was so shallow that no blood emerged. With all his strength and weight he pressed downward. Hisses of and steam from wounds sealing told him the sorcerer's arms had begun to heal. Once he dealt with Hargruss, Leoten needed to find Nerida and leave the base, but they wouldn't get far if the sorcerer got the chance to interfere again.

With a surge of strength, Hargruss pushed Leoten's hand to one side, carving a bright red gash across his pale chest. The blade stabbed deep into the sorcerer's chest but missed his heart. Hargruss produced an agonized shriek and his legs kicked under Leoten and he tossed him to one side.

Hargruss scrambled on his hands, dragging his wounded leg, he vanished behind the leaking tank in the center of the room. Tracks of blood from his cuts and gunshot wounds trailed behind him.

Leoten caught his breath. Beside him, Maia groaned and rolled onto her side. Aunwe crouched behind the lab desk where Hayin had fallen, her silhouette visible in the slight glow from the pile terminals.

"Fox," said Leoten. "Are you alright?"

Aunwe put a bloody hand on top of the lab table. "I'm alive."

"Hayin?" he asked.

Leoten's stomach twisted as Aunwe trembled and shook her head in reply.

A shape appeared by the leak in the tank at his side. The creature in the water examined the cracks in the glass as Leoten got to his feet and limped toward Aunwe and Hayin. He looked over his shoulder at Maia and the tank and returned his bloody signature knife to his bonded hand.

Aunwe rose from behind the table, the front of her suit dotted with blood. "She's gone, Red."

"I'm sorry." Leoten sank to the floor beside Maia. "Maia, are you all right?"

"My back," she said through a mouth made tight by pain. "I think I'll live."

"Fox," said Leoten. "Did you see where Nerida went?"

Aunwe shook her head. "We need to find her before we lose any other agents."

"What other agents are there, apart from the two of us?"

"The rest of my team is moving in from above," said Aunwe. "I don't know their exact location."

Maia pushed herself upright with a grunt. "I think I can walk."

"Good," said Leoten. "Let's hope we don't have to run."

Aunwe walked over to them, her hand pressed to the cut in her collar. She said nothing, but her mental presence betrayed her unease and grief to Leoten. He couldn't think of any lines of poetry or scripture to comfort her. Unwilling to give into powerlessness, he looked around for some means to stop the blood flow from the wound near her collar.

"Find Nerida." Aunwe waved off Leoten's offer to dress her wound. "I'll keep watch as long as I can while my team moves in."

"Just as long as they don't kill me when they see me," Leoten said.

Aunwe shook her head. "That monster, Hargruss, is our primary concern right now, and we share that." She clenched a fist to her chest.

"Agreed." Leoten turned to Maia. "Stay with Aunwe. I'm going to find Nerida." He drew his pistol and replaced the magazine with a full one from his mission case. He crept around the leaking tank, weapons bare but lowered.

· · · ·

CHAPTER 10

He hunted through the laboratory with the eyes of the creature in the tank following him. Not wanting to risk calling out Nerida's name, lest he alert Hargruss to her position, Leoten reached out with his mind instead. The flame magus was still nearby, so that meant she must not have been caught by any of the base's surviving staff or Hargruss's minions.

Leoten swept the barrel of his pistol over the floor, looking for signs of struggle amid the bloody trail Hargruss had left when he slithered away. That demon was different from the other creatures Leoten had fought from beyond the world.

Even Call's shoddok henchmen back in Volsokorod hadn't been so tough. But then, Hargruss had refused to serve Call, where the others had worked with him willingly. Could the sorcerer really be part of the Corporeum? That agency was rumored to exist across many distant realms, none of which Leoten or the TCR could confirm even existed. He'd only met one of their agents and the encounter had been brief and bloody.

A steel tile shifted ahead of him and he retreated a pace, gun rising in apprehension. "Who's there?" asked a muffled voice from below the floor.

"That's my question for you."

"Leoten?" Nerida rose from the crawlspace. Her red hair looked like copper in the dim light. "Did you finish Hargruss?" She turned toward him, hope in her eyes and the question fresh on her lips.

He shook his head. "He escaped. Do you think I can kill him?"

"I'm not sure," said Nerida. "All I know is what I felt when he attacked my mind. It was like everything just stopped, not at all like when you used your powers on me."

Leoten frowned. "We can worry about that later, but right now, we need to get out of this base."

"I know." Nerida sighed. "Are you working with Drufan?"

"Temporarily," said Leoten. "Aunwe and I have an understanding of how our current missions align."

"Is that the truth?"

"She's agreed with me so far."

Nerida climbed onto the floor at the same level as Leoten, but rather than standing up, she hesitated where she sat and wrapped her arms around herself. "Is everyone all right?"

"Hargruss killed Hayin. I don't know about most of the others outside these labs, but Maia and Aunwe will live. We left Volo in the docks, so he should be safe too."

"Sarah?" asked Nerida.

"Last I saw her she was alive. The same goes for Roy Chenn, the chief of security."

"Good. They're both decent people."

"Is there anyone else you want to extract?" Leoten asked.

Nerida looked at the floor. Shadows covered her face. "Some of the experimental specimens we created might still be alive."

"What level are they on?" he asked.

"Besides the strange one in the tank behind you," said Nerida. "They're all housed further down. Did you wonder why they needed so many blood magi and only one flame magus as scientists? It's because Maia and Volo had a lead that Crane was trying to follow. He must have been willing to hurt me because he thought I wasn't necessary any longer."

"You mean—What did you four accomplish at this base?"

"Idraster is more than test site. It's a cradle," said Nerida. "We must try to get to submersed level five before Hargruss and his people."

"What's on level five?"

"The subjects we infused with dragon's blood," said Nerida. "They've given me all the hope I could want, especially after Volskorod, and what happened to Henry and the Iron Dragon there."

"These subjects...Are they human?"

"Yes. Despite Crane's best efforts."

"You mean—"

"He wanted to create dragon spawn, but after we distilled the dragon's blood through the most stringent titration it eventually came out silver."

"Silver blood?"

"Crane called it Sokiaster. It's a word from an original version of one of the Books of Becoming."

A chill ran through Leoten like he'd suffered a rush of fever. "A copy of the Books of Becoming was a component to summon Hargruss to our world. A particular page was torn out and burned but I don't know which one."

Nerida hung her head. "Whatever I've done, I've done in the name of justice. I want to protect the innocent, not destroy them as he does."

Leoten scowled. "So he is a demon like I suspected."

"Perhaps." Nerida raised her head and then extended her arm to Leoten.

He helped her to her feet. "I'll help you rescue the subjects from level five. I promise I won't let another disaster happen like back in Volskorod."

"Don't say that." Nerida's lips trembled, and she pressed a hand to her forehead.

"Say what?"

"Don't make a promise you can't keep," she said.

He squeezed her hand gently, then released his grip altogether. "Aunwe and Maia are back the way we came."

"Do you truly trust Aunwe?" asked Nerida.

"Yes."

"How can you? She works for the DGD."

"She has honor of her own." He leaned close to Nerida's ear. "And we share a secret, though it's mine to tell."

"What secret?" she whispered.

"The dragon from Volskorod died in the vault," he said in a low voice. "But not completely. I saved his mind."

Nerida shoved him gently backward, then matched him gaze to gaze with a serious expression. "You're not trying to trick me, are you?"

"I wouldn't lie about that to you."

"You're too honest to be a spy."

"My father says the same thing sometimes." He motioned her toward the front of the tank where Aunwe and Maia waited. "Go ahead. I'll watch our backs."

Her eyes closed for a moment and she took a deep breath. "Leoten, I want to trust you."

"You can. That's a promise I'll keep, no matter what."

She hesitated a moment longer, then threw her arms around his neck. "I didn't think you'd come. I thought...I thought I'd never be able to show anyone I cared for about what I've made." She sobbed into his chest. "Thank you."

He clapped a hand to her back, then with a few coaxing steps, started to back toward the front of the tank and the laboratory complex.

• • • •

THEY REJOINED AUNWE and Maia. Aunwe placed a white coat from one of the access lockers over Hayin's still form. She turned toward Leoten and Nerida, who now walked side by side. Occasionally she leaned against his shoulder for support, though otherwise, she seemed surer on her feet than Leoten felt.

"Red," said Aunwe. "You found her."

"Yeah." Leoten looked over his shoulder. "But Hargruss is still alive. I didn't follow his trail long enough to catch up and finish him."

"Good," said Aunwe. "That monster isn't for you alone to kill." Her eyes looked crimson at the rims from tears, or from fighting them.

"I know," he said.

Maia turned to Nerida. "We made it."

"So far," Nerida's gaze lingered on the white coat that covered Hayin's body. "But not all of us can say so."

Aunwe blinked and turned to Nerida. "Hayin was an agent of the DGD. She was in deep cover here at Idraster to keep an eye on the rest of you."

"I never would have guessed," said Nerida. "She was kind to me."

Maia nodded. "She was kind to all of us. It feels wrong to leave her here."

"We from Drufan don't believe the spirit lingers long with our remains," said Aunwe. "She's left this place ahead of us, and she'd tell you the same if she could speak."

Leoten bowed his head. "Fair words, though the Triumvirate clerics would dispute them. I've never cared much for their kind, regardless."

Maia sighed. "You two must be used to losing friends. I'm sorry, but I'm not."

"It's not something that ever stops hurting," said Aunwe.

Leoten nodded. "But we need to move on." He glanced at Nerida. "What's the best way to get to level five from here if we don't use the service elevator? I have a feeling Hargruss will have that under guard."

"We could try the filter pipe," said Maia. "They use the mirrors in it to bounce natural light to the lower levels."

"All the way to the lowest." Nerida nodded. "I think you're right, Maia. But we need to find a way to get to Volo first."

"Not yet," said Leoten. "He's still in the docks at level three and should be safe even if they find him. After all, he's the only magus Hargruss might be able to capture for the moment."

"Don't be so certain he'll be safe, though," said Aunwe. "We don't know what the demon planned to do with Maia and Nerida if we hadn't intervened."

Maia turned to Nerida. "Actually, I remember something. I was almost awake. He said something before he attacked my mind and knocked me out."

"What did he say?" asked Nerida.

The blood magus folded her arms. "I only remember a few words," she said. "But he repeated one sentence at least twice."

Leoten leaned toward Maia.

She said, "He chanted them. It sounded like an incantation and a request for someone I couldn't see to help. His chant went like this," Maia took a deep breath, then continued, "Bind us to each other. Mind touches mind. We form the Touchwork." She sighed. "He repeated the last two sentences, I think."

"Mind touches mind?" said Aunwe. "Sounds like an incantation, for certain. Red?"

"It's nothing I learned in the Temple of Colors," said Leoten. "I suspect he didn't gain his mind-eater powers the way I learned mine."

Nerida explained the difference between Leoten and Hargruss's mental attacks. "It's like my thoughts turned static," she said. "Paused in motion like a stopped pile recording."

"Damn it," said Maia. "I felt the same way."

Aunwe and Leoten locked eyes. "Whatever he was doing," she said. "He intended only evil."

"Agreed," said Leoten.

"I can retrieve Volo, then catch up with you," said Aunwe. "As much as I hate to say it, that may be our best move.

"We must move as one," said Nerida.

Leoten glanced at the red-haired flame magus. "I agree with Nerida." He turned to her. "We'll do this together."

· · · ·

CHAPTER 11

Hargruss's wounds steamed as they healed before Joachim's eyes. The sorcerer had propped his back against the bulkhead by the elevator doors. His odd, glassy eyes gazed into space as if death had managed to claim him, despite all other evidence pointing to the contrary.

"Captain Zodai," said a voice from one of the soldiers nearby.

Joachim massaged his aching neck and upper back, while he pressed his other palm to his forehead. The mental attack by the agent called Red had left him paralyzed for a time. Only Hargruss had ever hit him that hard before and freeze him for seconds like an elongated electrical jolt.

"Captain Zodai?"

"What?" snapped Joachim.

"They're coming this way, sir."

"Who?"

"The enemy agents and the magi we'd captured."

Joachim stifled a sigh. "We need to move or fight. Don't think Hargruss or our employer will be of any help right now."

One of the bolder troopers reached for Hargruss's arm to help him up.

Hargruss rasped an alien curse from the corner of his shark-like mouth. "I can stand on my own, soldier." He retrieved a leather pouch from his belt. "And I will move when I must."

The young mercenary retreated from the sorcerer. Her eyes darted to Joachim. "Sir?"

Joachim got to his feet. "People, we are leaving this area. We'll regroup on level one and await further orders."

The trooper who'd reached for Hargruss, Lucia of the Gadal Household, nodded. "What about our charge?"

"Leave me here, soldier. That will be fine." Hargruss snorted and blood flecked his lips. "I alone am enough." He sprinkled white sand from the pouch in his hand onto the floor around him in a semi-circle.

"Enough for what?" asked Joachim.

"Enough to ensure Mister Vorsei isn't disappointed in our efforts," said Hargruss. "Now, go. Or do you and your soldiers want to die here, Captain Zodai?"

Joachim listened. He learned. He obeyed.

• • • •

LEOTEN APPROACHED THE darkened intersection by the elevator doors. He halted as the sight in the gloom before him resolved itself into the pallid skeletal form of Hargruss. The sorcerer sat cross-legged, his back to the wall beside the elevator. Faint silver flickers from his steaming wounds were the only source of light from the front. Nerida's candleflame illuminated a semicircle of sand that cut the sorcerer off from Leoten's mental sense. Hargruss' hands rested on his knees and his eyes were closed.

"I didn't sense his spirit." Aunwe hissed.

"What is he doing?" Nerida asked.

Leoten scowled. "Meditating? We don't know enough."

"We never do," said Nerida.

As she spoke, Hargruss raised his head. Strange yellow eyes opened and a harsh, thick breath issued from his mouth and misted in the air before him.

"Are you awake?" asked Leoten.

"I want to talk with you," said Hargruss, "Leoten Seol."

"Do you have a surname?" asked Leoten.

"No." The small cloud of breath before Hargruss distorted as he spoke and then shifted to resemble two spheres, one contained inside the other. "I was born far away." He motioned to the sphere. "On a parched world beneath a liquid sky."

Beside Leoten, Nerida frowned. He didn't need to touch her mind to know she was considering the possible meanings of his words.

Aunwe trembled. One hand fell to the pistol she held at her belt, fully loaded. No doubt she wished to dispatch the demon for his murder of Hayin.

"I've never heard of such a place," said Leoten.

"They don't appear in the Books of Being," said Maia. "At least, I don't think they do."

"They wouldn't, Maia Zami." Hargruss's cloud of breath warped into a smooth ovoid, like an eggshell but with thin lines that traced its surface. And within the egg a human body lay in a fetal curl. "Nor do they mention my kind, born as we are between mortals and gods."

"What are you?" Aunwe sounded hoarse.

"I'm no foe of dragons and no friend to Shoddok."

"Yet, you're a killer..." she said.

"You three came to kill me." Hargruss sighed. "But time is too short to argue philosophy."

"Why is time short?"

"Ewatti Vorsei is on his way to Idraster. If anyone is going to save what grows in the levels below we must hurry. I have a feeling he won't like what he finds."

Nerida stepped forward. "We can't work with you."

"I know." Hargruss closed his eyes. "And Zodai's mercenaries would prove a nuisance rather an asset to my safety if I let them know what I'm telling you now."

"Why are you telling us all this?" asked Leoten.

"So you'll learn," said Hagruss. "The Corporeum is not a unified organization. I stand to gain much if I can return with the information I've gained."

"You didn't come here by choice?" Leoten said. "Call summoned you to Fyon with a ritual."

"A sacrifice of fire and blood," said Hargruss. "And in doing so he bound me with only part of my powers. I have no way to contact my allies beyond as I am now."

Maia's eyes widened and she stepped forward. "You were going to kill me to reconstruct your ability, weren't you?"

"Yes."

Nerida's eyes flashed and she formed a series of sigils in the air with her hands. A stream of her magical flames erupted and burned toward Hargruss. Their light seared across Leoten's eyes. When the fire reached the barrier of sand on the floor it curved around the air above the circle, but didn't pierce the mystic shell.

"Counter magic?" Aunwe scowled.

"I knew you'd be hostile," said Hargruss. "I see this conversation is finished."

"Right," said Leoten. "Everyone, get to the elevator before the flames die down."

Maia nodded, then ran to the doors. Aunwe stalked after her, machine pistol trained on Hargruss. Her finger twitched in and out of the trigger guard. Nerida and Leoten brought up the rear as the elevator doors opened. He didn't feel any safer until the doors closed and they descended toward the Locust dock.

• • • •

WITHIN THE DOCK, VOLO leaned against the wall by the doors, waiting for them. "You did it," he said. "Where's Hayin?"

Maia shook her head.

Volo's face turned pale. "No." He looked at his feet. "How could they?"

Nerida glanced at Leoten.

Aunwe stepped out of the car on his other side. "Too easily." She grimaced. "I don't know how, but I need to kill Hargruss."

"We'd all be better off if you could." Nerida folded her arms. "But first, we need to get to the lower levels and rescue the subjects."

Leoten nodded to Volo. "I won't ask you to go deeper into the base. But it will be safer if we stick together."

The magus wiped tears from his eyes, then rubbed his bald patch. "I don't want to slow you all down."

"You won't," said Nerida. "And we'll need your help, Volo."

"Why?" he asked. "Hayin was always the better shaper."

"Well," said Nerida. "We don't have Hayin."

Maia took a step toward Volo. "She's right. I'm not half the shaper either you or Hayin are. Were. Damn it!"

Leoten started along the wall, looking for another exit to the dock. The elevator doors closed and the lift departed. "Sorry, but you don't have long to think things over."

"We'll use the service corridor to get to the stairs," said Volo. "I'll lead the way."

"Thanks," said Leoten.

They followed Volo down a flight of stairs on one side of the catwalk. Aunwe moved slower than the others. She still carried her bonded pistol and occasionally looked over her shoulder at the doors behind them. Leoten waited for a moment for her to catch up with him. He put a hand on her arm and leaned close to her.

"You won't win alone if you fight them," he said.

"You don't know that."

"I'd call it a good guess."

She lowered her head, then shrugged off his hand. "I'll be all right. I just can't believe he would kill her so casually, then act as if it wasn't somehow personal."

"I understand," said Leoten. "And everything he's said so far only raised further questions for me."

"If I can avoid killing him, I should try. But we need to hurry." Aunwe placed the machine pistol in a makeshift gun sling at her hip. "I'll control myself until the time is right."

"Good."

"Leoten?"

"Yeah?"

She leaned close to him, so he felt her brush against his chest. "I appreciate that you care."

Their gazes locked. "It's odd because you're a Drufanesh agent, but I do."

"I know." She patted his arm, then slipped away. Leoten followed her and the others into the passage that led from the dock deeper into Idraster Base.

They descended to level four, but the staircase ended there. "It's to keep enemies from getting to the bottom at speed during an attack," said Volo. "Crane told me that once."

Leoten frowned. "So they predicted an attack? Here?"

"It seems so," said Aunwe. "I believe the designers must have known the level of danger their research brought to them and the rest of the Otrusia." She peered around the side of the doorway leading out of the narrow stairwell, then ducked back. "There's someone in the passage."

"I didn't see anyone," said Volo.

"Eyes can't tell you everything. There is someone there."

"Who?"

"A strong spirit, a man alone." Aunwe frowned. "I don't recognize him."

Leoten approached the doorway. "Roy?" he called. "is that you out there?"

"Red?" said the security chief from a side passage a few meters away. "How did you know?"

"Just a hunch," said Leoten. "We're not here to fight."

"Gods, I hope you're telling the truth," Roy said. "Seems like I wouldn't do well against five magi on my own."

"Reasonable," said Leoten.

"I like that." Aunwe touched Leoten's forearm. "Roy, have yous seen mercenaries on this level?"

"A few came in through the vents." The security chief stepped into the passage before them. "I don't know where they are now."

"Or how many came down." Maia exchanged rueful looks with Nerida.

"Where are you going?" Roy asked. "I thought you'd bug out as soon as you got the magi together."

"That was the plan." Leoten smirked for an instant. "But you know how plans go."

"Shit." Roy ducked against the wall by the corner of the passage where he'd just been hiding. A few cracks of gunfire rang out from further down the way. He looked at Leoten, Aunwe, and the magi. "Damn, but these mercs are right on top of us."

Aunwe stepped forward and raised her pistol. "Not for long."

Nerida nodded. "We'll handle this."

They approached the entrance of the side passage. Aunwe closed her eyes. "I count four of them, two on the left and two on the right."

"I've got the right, then." Nerida's fury flared in her eyes.

"I'll take the left." Aunwe hugged the wall of the side passage and fired a burst from her pistol at the enemies out of sight. Nerida conjured an orb of fire and then hurled it along the passageway. Distant screams answered their attack but no shots retaliated.

Efficient, Leoten thought, *they work well together.* He, Volo, and Maia joined them along with Roy. They started along the passage they'd just secured.

"Have the subjects on Level Five moved?" asked Nerida.

Roy shrugged. "Not that I know. Protocol is to keep them as far from combat as possible."

"We'll follow that rule as long as we can," Nerida said. "Security Chief Chenn, did you see what happened to the inspectors?"

He shook his head. "I got separated from everyone else after that monster breached the ceiling on Level One. Thought I could head off the action if I rushed down here."

"We'll have more company soon," said Aunwe. "I sense many spirits descending."

Leoten reached out with his mind. Minds both familiar and unfamiliar scurried down stairways, crept through vents, and rode on elevator cars. Everyone above raced deeper and deeper into the base. She was right, but Aunwe probably didn't know how completely.

He turned to Roy. "What's the fastest way to move to the lower levels?"

The man met his eyes but said nothing for a long moment.

Hargruss. Sarah. Vorsei's mercenaries.

The possible obstacles to their escape would only increase the longer they took to reach any experimental subjects. Roy hesitated with Leoten's eyes locked on him.

"Look," he said. "You can tell, me, or I can ransack your mind for the information I need."

"I'm thinking," said Roy. "That's all. There." He pointed down the narrow side passage from where they stood. "There's an air shaft on the other side of the wall there and an access hatch to get to it. It might be three or four meters to Level Five from there."

"Perfect." Leoten's brows bent. "Lead the way, security chief."

"Wait." Aunwe held up a hand. "I relayed our position to my backup team. They'll be here in ten minutes."

"We're under twenty meters of ice and water," said Nerida. "How are your agents going to reach us at all?"

"I don't feel like turning myself over to Drufan today," said Volo. Maia nodded.

Aunwe grimaced. "I've told them to go deeper. They can meet us on Level Five."

Leoten looked from each to the others, then down the passage toward the air shaft. "Go ahead, Roy."

He only hoped Aunwe's team wouldn't come in ready to shoot him. No matter who the opponent might be, a battle so deep underwater might be one of their worst options.

● ● ● ●

CHAPTER 12

Leoten advanced toward the source of the mental pulse. Aunwe was close behind him, her pistol in hand, but Nerida reached for the Drufanesh agent's hand as she went to load the weapon. "That won't be necessary, Fox."

"Why not?" asked Aunwe.

"Because I can sense her fire boiling from within. That mind and spirit you sense belong to our most advanced subject."

Leoten kept his eyes forward. "What kind of subject is she?"

"Class K," said Nerida. "Her body has been remade with dragon's blood and living pile matter. Her name is Viv."

"I hear her now," said Aunwe. "She's calling out for help."

The lights above them flickered. Hargruss's presence struck Leoten and the world began to slow. *Damn. He followed us faster than I thought he would.* Leoten croaked out a warning but couldn't hear his voice. Gray ripples filled the edge of his vision and then he felt himself frozen and cold, paralyzed in a dream.

Hargruss. Demon.
Aunwe. Light.
Nerida. Hope.

The dead lingered close to the surface, among flickers of grainy static. His limbs tingled. Leoten rolled onto his side. Aunwe lay on her back beside him but he couldn't see Nerida or any of the others. Hargruss may have paralyzed them all with his power.

The demon could be on top of them any minute and Leoten couldn't even speak or move his toes.

Doom came, he thought, *and not a doom worthy of a few good verses of poetry.*

"It won't end here for you," said a serene voice from within him. After months of silence, he recognized the mind of the Iron Dragon that brushed against his consciousness. His fingers and toes twitched. He moved with effort, pushing himself to his feet. As he'd feared, everyone else slumped on the cold metal floor, except for Nerida, who stood ahead of him, halfway down the passage.

"What the hell is happening?" she asked.

"It's Hargruss." Leoten gritted his teeth. "He's coming." He crouched beside Aunwe. Her eyes were closed and her breathing moved her chest in and out. Leoten slipped an arm around her waist and dragged her from the floor. Volo, Maia, and Roy would have to hold on. He'd be back for them.

Leoten carried Aunwe over his shoulder as he marched toward Nerida. She stood, frozen. "We can't abandon the others."

"We won't leave them for long. We need Viv and the others to fight back."

Nerida bit her lip as though she'd meant to object, but then nodded. She led the way for Leoten on the path to the test subject's room. He prayed they could convince Viv to fight before Hargruss arrived.

A wave of paralyzing static hit Leoten from Hargruss's mental strike, nothing at all like an ordinary mind-eater. The dragon within Leoten kept him mobile. He caught up with Nerida by the hatchway. Aunwe still hung, body limp, over his shoulder, but her fingers twitched against his back as Nerida knocked on the door.

"Viv," said Nerida.

"Nerida?" came a girl's voice from within the room. "What's going on?"

"Too much to explain. We have to get off of Idraster."

"They locked down all of us, test subjects." A low snarl from within the room followed those words. "If I break the door I'll be in trouble."

Boots pounded in the passage behind them, approaching the corner where Maia, Volo, and Roy still lay paralyzed.

Nerida leaned close to the door. "Things are worse than that kind of trouble. You have to do it."

Viv sighed with guttural frustration. "Fine. Stand back."

Two of Hargruss's mercenaries round the corner and leveled their automatic rifles at Leoten, Nerida, and Aunwe. "Hands up. Don't any of you magi try anything or we'll shoot." The man's finger hovered nervously just outside the trigger guard.

A volley of shots exploded down the passage, making Nerida and Leoten duck and cringe against Viv's sealed hatch. But they hadn't been the targets. Both mercenaries dropped with gurgles of blood. The gunfire died with them. Leoten propped Aunwe against the door frame as she began to return to her senses.

"Thanks," she said.

"It's nothing." Leoten put a hand on her shoulder, then turned to look over his shoulder to find the shooter. "Sarah."

She stood with a long machine rifle in both hands. "Don't move, Leoten. Don't make me shoot you, too."

He nodded. "I won't make you do anything. But he kept his grip on Aunwe's upper arm and caught her eye. Her spirit carried his mind forth and their powers rushed Sarah. Projected by Aunwe's magic, Leoten devoured Sarah's aggression with savage speed. He left her awake but she lowered her weapon in numbed fingers. He grimaced. "Nerida, the door."

"Viv, we're alright for now," Nerida said. "Come out or we might all die down here."

The footfalls of more mercenaries pounded in the passage behind them, followed by the languid, ominous gait of Hargruss himself. Sarah ducked out of sight on the other side, but her mind remained close.

"Damn," Leoten rose from his crouch and lifted the barrel of his pistol. "Here they come. "Guess we may not get a chance to meet up with your team after all, Aunwe."

She got to her feet with a tremor in her legs. "It's fine." The Drufanesh agent touched his arm and linked her spirit's reach with his mind magic. They marched down the passage toward the intersection. Behind them, Nerida retreated and the hatchway buckled, then burst open. Bolts and metal plates rattled against the opposite wall. Leoten and Aunwe looked over their shoulders as Viv emerged, a burnt-umber-haired young human woman with dragon's fire smoldering in her mouth.

Hargruss stepped into the passage past the fallen mercenaries. He ignored everything else as he sank to one knee beside Maia's head. His rictus grin looked angled toward her face. His eyes never blinked.

Leoten took a step toward them and then felt Aunwe's hand on his arm.

She spoke one word, "Together."

His pistol in one hand and his signature knife in the other, Leoten couldn't reach for her, but he might other have done so in that wild moment. Her spiritual warmth flooded into his mind. Perhaps their battle with Hargruss would be worthy of a few secret lines of poetry, but he doubted either of them would live to see.

• • • •

CHAPTER 13

Witnesses of a mental battle might find each move difficult to notice at first, but Leoten's attention focused with needle-like precision for each strike and parry. Combined with Aunwe's spirit for speed and reach, he stabbed, pried, and hammered at Hargruss's cold and death-like outer defenses.

Each time, the sorcerer from beyond the world struck back and forced them to retreat. All the while Leoten and Aunwe marched along the passage toward where the demon knelt over Maia, Roy, and Volo.

Just five meters from Hargruss, Leoten struck deep into his enemy's subconscious, piercing the rigid shell that guarded the alien mind. His stay in the interior would last only seconds, so he scrambled to defend as Aunwe implanted an aversion to the handle of the magic sword Hargruss carried. He would have to dig out that false thought before he could kill them with the blade.

Hargruss coughed and steam issued from his mouth. Yellow eyes fix on Maia's face. She stared, paralyzed, perhaps not even able to see the monstrous face before her. Hargruss wrapped the fingers of one skeletal hand around her collar and dragged her toward him even as his inner defenses repulsed Leoten and Aunwe from his mind.

Leoten hissed an intake of breath and then lunged at Hargruss with his signature knife. The sorcerer's right hand held Maia's collar and his left struggled to reach for his sword, but fingers always stopped short of the weapon's hilt.

The knife descended toward the demon's unprotected neck.

A single finger flicked out from the left hand and a punch of force hit Leoten in the chest. The telekinetic blow made him stagger to one side and his strike carved a path along Hargruss's shoulder blade rather than plunge into his spine. The demon's wound began to steam at once, the same pale white color as the gas that billowed from his open mouth.

"What is that steam?" shouted Nerida from behind them.

Leoten had the same question, but no answer.

A rod of what looked like porous, hardened black chitin emerged from Hargruss's throat. It glistened in the glow from the passage's electric lights.

Aunwe left Leoten's side. Her leg rose and her heel fell like a guillotine that crashed into Hargruss's neck. The blow drove the demonic enemy to the floor. He seethed as the slender chitin rod rolled out of his grip.

Leoten holstered his pistol and reached for the half-meter length of darkness.

"No!" Hargruss rasped. "Don't touch it!"

Aunwe lashed out with her other foot to connect with his chin. Hargruss's head snapped upward and blood ran from his mouth. "Ignore him, Red."

Hargruss retreated in a crouch. He wiped the trickle of blood that ran down his jaw. "A curse upon you, Aunwe Reomi," he said. "For that, I'll take your head." The demon's fingers found a grip on his sword by avoiding the hilt and grasping the naked blade so the edge cut into his palm and drew blood.

Leoten scooped up the black rod and found the material warm and slick to the touch. Despite his disgust, he grasped the instrument tight.

"You don't know what you've done." Hargruss lifted the flowing length of his sword from his back. His lanky frame unfolded as he rose. "Regardless, you've earned an enemy's death, Leoten Seol."

The black chitinous rod hung loose in Leoten's fingers, surprisingly lightweight. He wondered for a moment what he could do with the repulsive thing. Nerida shouted from behind him. "Red! Here!"

A real magus would have a better idea of how to handle an artifact of unknown use like the black rod. He whirled and tossed the length of chitin underhand. Viv stepped forward in front of Nerida and snatched the strange artifact from the air.

"Perfect," said Nerida. "Viv, your fire should be able to destroy it."

"No!" Hargruss shrieked. He lashed out with both hands, one empty but for his telekinetic magic, and the other wrapped around the blade of his sword tight enough for blood to flow from both fingers and palm.

Aunwe and Leoten threw themselves sideways and then forward. They came at Hargruss from opposite directions. The demon's sword slashed through the air toward Viv and Nerida, but appeared unable to twist or maneuver with precision at such long range. Viv held out the rod between herself and the sword's point. The strike froze in mid-air. The rush of Hargruss's magic made Viv's thin tunic and pants ripple, but lacked the force to hurl her away.

Hargruss snarled and began to withdraw his blade. Leoten's signature knife slipped between the demon's ribs. Aunwe delivered two swift kicks, the first to Hargruss's chin, the second to the hilt of Leoten's blade to drive it deeper. He released his grip and let the knife fulfill its purpose.

The sorcerer's gales of force faded to an unnatural but gentle breeze and his yellow eyes closed. Hargruss slumped to the floor between Maia and Volo. His sword's blade slithered back to the shape it held while at rest, even as the weapon rolled from limp white fingers.

Volo sat up with a groan. "Damn. What happened?"

"We killed him." Aunwe nodded to Leoten. "Now, we need to get out of here."

Leoten checked Hargruss for a pulse in the neck but found none. That might not prove as much as it would in a human, but it gave him hope. He looked down the passageway at where Sarah had disappeared. "We need to get out of Idraster Base." He raised his voice. "Nerida, is there anyone else we should take with us?"

"Viv?" asked Nerida.

"I don't think the other subjects are willing. They listen to the propaganda all day and like it."

"One will have to be enough," said Leoten.

"I understand." Aunwe helped Maia to her feet. She and Leoten looked down at Roy as the security chief recovered from Hargruss's static paralysis. Aunwe loaded her machine pistol.

"No need for that," said Roy. "Just go. I'll tell my surviving people to stand down."

"You'll be court-marshaled for that," said Leoten.

"Only if they can catch me." Roy grinned. "I don't plan to make that easy."

Leoten cracked a small smile, then turned to Aunwe. She shouldered her weapon. "We may still have mercenaries between us and the surface, Red."

He shrugged. "For their sake, I hope they don't get in our way."

• • • •

THEY RACED, UNHINDERED, to the cargo elevator in the locust dock on submersible level three. As they rode upward toward level two klaxons began to blare through the base. "As if we didn't have enough trouble," said Nerida.

Viv's lips drew back in a snarl.

"What's wrong?" asked Aunwe.

"That's the air-warning. We've got another unexpected locust overhead."

"Could it be one of yours from the Triumvirate?" Aunwe asked Leoten.

He scowled. "No."

• • • •

CHAPTER 14

His boot splashed in water from leaks as Joachim Zodai crouched for cover behind an overturned table on the first level. His survivors blind-fired from cover to keep the Otrusian security troops' in hiding.

Hargruss was out of contact. Whatever that could mean, it wasn't good for business. His fire teams consisted of fine fighters, but they came to back the sorcerer's moves, not conquer Idraster on their own. He pulled the pin on a burst grenade and then hurled it over-handed. A round from Private Lucia's bonded pistol hit the bomb as it began to fall between two clusters of Otrusians. The grenade exploded with a roar and the recursive whine of scattering shrapnel. The enemy fire died away.

The way out was clear.

"Everyone, no more nonsense! We're leaving this wretched base." Joachim's order found eager ears. They ran past the shredded and ruined bodies of security troops and reached the tower door. Joachim slapped each trooper on the back as they passed him and continued up the stairs to the cold air outside.

Lucia scurried to the exit just one flight of stairs up. She glanced back at him. "The Locust is still here. We made it!"

"Finally some gods-damned good news." Joachim checked behind him, then started up the stairs only to stop, frozen on the first step. A static pulse crackled repeatedly within his mind. His mouth slowly sounded out the name of his fear. "Har. Gruss."

"I'm alive, Commander Zodai. Tell your people to impede Red's escape or I'll see to it you never leave this base alive." The voice in his mind didn't come out as a rasp but as a death rattle. "Are we clear, Zodai?"

Not at all. Not by the damnedest sight ever seen outside the Books of the Prophets.

"Yourself and the private near you will be enough. Slow the enemy down for two minutes until I can join you." The sorcerer released Joachim from the static.

"Private," he said to Lucia. "You're with me. We've got to keep anyone from following us."

"What?" Lucia's brows bent inward above her balaclava. "Sir, we're clear to leave."

"Not yet." Joachim grunted in frustration. "We have one last mission on this base. Just us two are enough for it."

Lucia rushed down the steps and fixed him with an intense gaze. "Was it him, sir?"

He nodded. "To hell with Hargruss, but he's alive. We need to slow the enemy agents down for two minutes. He'll let us go after that."

She shook her head. "I'll watch your back, sir. But I won't die for that monster."

Joachim clapped her on the shoulder. "We won't. That's a promise."

• • • •

THE MAGES RUSHED UP the stairs to a passage that passed by the mess hall on the first level of the base. Leoten led the way. Nerida moved among the others, keeping pace as she offered words of encouragement to Maia, Volo, and Viv. Aunwe brought up the rear, looking pale and going light on her wounded leg. The fight with Hargruss may have drained her even more than it fatigued Leoten. She only lagged by a few meters, but that could be critical in a dangerous situation.

The halls they passed were derelict and leaked icy salt water. Leoten waved the others forward, while he moved back along the line to make sure Aunwe didn't fall too far behind.

What am I doing, he thought. *She's an agent of Drufan. We can't both win this time or most times for that matter.* He gazed down the passage behind them and found it as empty as the way ahead. They needed to get to the tower to reach the surface. If that didn't work, the sea runner den might provide a decent chance at an alternate escape route. However, that would be riskier as only he and Aunwe were dressed for the cold water.

She met his eyes. "Don't worry about me, Red."

"I can't help it."

Her cheeks flushed. "You must. They need you more." She motioned to Nerida, Viv, Maia, and Volo. "They are your mission, not me."

"I haven't forgotten."

"I didn't mean to say you had."

"I mean, I haven't forgotten about Volskorod. The vault."

"There's no time for this, Red."

He bit his tongue to keep back a rapid retort. *Will there ever be time?* He thought the words rather than said them, despite the cliche in them that would violate even the most perfect verse by its presence.

"Go ahead." Aunwe limped by his side. "Keep them safe for the sake of the world. For all of us."

"Fox, I understand. I only—"

"You don't have to tell me." She squeezed his hand. The icy trickles of water on the walls around them ceased their downward flow and spread into feathered patterns that described the shapes of hands clasped together, each one a pair where half belonged to her and the other half to him. Her powers manifested strangely at times. He'd witnessed it before. That thought offered comfort for a moment, along with her warm touch. She released her grip and Leoten moved forward.

He took the lead ahead of Nerida and Viv just as a smoking irritant gas grenade rolled out of a side corridor a meter ahead of them.

"Hold your breath as long as you can and close your eyes. Everyone, link with your neighbors and form a chain." Leoten grasped Nerida's hand, and led the group forward through the smoke. As the leader, only he couldn't afford to move forward blind. Just twenty meters to the tower door and they slowed to a crawl.

He scanned the passage ahead of them as tears beaded in his eyes from the gas. He favored his signature knife ready to throw, rather than count on his service pistol with all the water about. They passed across the last T-shaped intersection before the tower door ten meters away.

"We're nearly there." Leoten's voice came out as a croak from the irritant in his throat. He released Nerida's hand and then guided her to grip Viv's fingers in place of his. "Open your eyes and breathe if you need it, but we need to keep going."

He moved back along the line

The passage around them was full of opaque white gas, but the others kept moving. Viv coughed and a spark flared from her mouth. Maia followed, with her lab coat pulled over her nose and mouth. Volo gasped for a breath as he guided Aunwe after Maia. Despite her obvious pain and discomfort, Aunwe moved like a dancer, a martial artist with precise muscular control.

The resounding blast of a gunshot broke through the cloying pain of the gas that filled his mouth and nose. Volo twisted with a scream as a bullet ripped through the elbow of the arm that he was using to guide Aunwe. The magus released Maia and Aunwe and clutched at his wound. Leoten tried to shout a warning to tell the others to get low, but his voice came out as a hiss and a cough. He scanned the side passage for the shooter but saw only impenetrable tear fog.

Nerida and Viv reached the tower door and turned back. Leoten grunted and dropped low against the floor. He banished his blade, then threw Volo's smaller frame across his back. Leoten rose to seek Aunwe with his free hand.

She took him by his seal suit's sleeve. The three of them stumbled after Maia as she left the billowing gas behind. Viv darted into the tower stairway while Nerida waited by the door, tracing sigils with both hands.

Leoten carried Volo to the door with Aunwe at his side. Another burst of gunfire sounded from somewhere in the distance. As the gas began to thin in the passage, a too-familiar alien mind pulsed hatred from the opposite end of the hall by the elevator.

"No. He must be dead. We killed him." Leoten's voice came out haltingly, a curse in his very being. "Hargruss is here."

Nerida's eyes widened. She stopped her spell preparation and grabbed Maia. She dragged the other magus through the hatchway door and into the tower.

A blast of cold magic-driven wind hit Leoten, Volo, and Aunwe and hurled them along the passage past the tower and the exit. Leoten skidded painfully on his knees. Metal plates tore at his seal suit, but he managed to stop himself just a meter from the doorway with Volo held over his shoulder while Aunwe pressed her back against the opposite wall.

Hargruss lowered his hand and marched toward them. The wounds in his chest and sword hand still steamed with his healing magic. The venomous curse Hargruss hurled after Leoten kept him from rising for longer than he could afford. He clenched his teeth and forced himself to stand, supported against the wall. His fingers clawed to find the door handle and, after a few seconds, reached it.

Aunwe released a burst of rounds from her pistol that rattled around Hargruss. One bullet cut his cheek. Another blew through the shoulder above his sword arm. The demonic sorcerer grinned like the face of death itself. He reached for the deadly sword on his back. Hargruss swung the weapon and released the blade to grow like jagged lightning toward Aunwe.

Leoten burst into motion with all his strength. He dropped Volo inside the tower doorway and then hurled himself into the sword's path. Hargruss's silver blade carved a gash in his right shoulder. Leoten staggered from the force and collided with Aunwe behind him. They both fell to the floor and he rolled off of her. The lethal blade twisted, and then retracted for the next strike.

He stared into the yellow eyes of the sorcerer as Hargruss stalked closer. The blade of his sword twisted like an eel, slick with fresh blood from Leoten's wound. Aunwe groaned. Her back pushed against the wall and her bonded pistol lay out of reach. The flowing serpentine metal of the sword coiled over Leoten, less than a meter from Aunwe.

But the point ignored him and turned toward her. Hargruss cackled. "I'll have your head yet, Fox."

He clenched his grip on the hilt of the sword and the blade drew back like an asp. Leoten growled in his throat as he summoned his signature knife, but his wounded shoulder wouldn't allow him to throw the weapon in time.

Aunwe, he thought. *I wish I could say I'm sorry for how things are turning out and have it mean anything at all.*

A sword's point thrust forth from a deep wound as it emerged from the front of Hargruss's chest. The sorcerer's chest wound steamed from the front and the back. Sarah stood behind him, her bonded blade wielded in both hands. The demon fell to his knees. Hearts-blood spilled onto the dusty, cold metal of the floor.

Leoten lurched to his feet and offered Aunwe his hand. Sarah gave him a single nod, then backed into the corridor beside where Hargruss now slumped, paralyzed in a deathlike stillness. Leoten and Sarah supported each other and they staggered into the tower and up the stairs to join the others at the surface.

Arctic sunlight shimmered through the fuzz of static-gray clouds. A locust circled overhead. Another slithered off the slick top of Idraster and into the frigid sea. Neither bore any markings, which meant that neither belonged to official government forces. But on the opposite side of the base from where the locust had begun to swim, the Triumvirate light cruiser that had escorted Leoten to Idraster floated close to the base. A smaller pile boat kicked the water into foam as it sped from the cruiser toward the base's side.

"Nerida," said Leoten, voice cracking from the pain and the residue of the gas. "That's our ride out of here." He pointed toward the ship.

The flame magus nodded. Maia shivered as the icy wind picked up. Viv adjusted Volo on her shoulders.

"Go," Leoten said. "Everyone."

They went into motion along the shallow surface water of the base. The tide was low, praise be, so the water wasn't high enough to get inside their shoes.

Aunwe turned to him. "Red. Thank you, but I have my own way out of here."

"I know." He gazed into her eyes, a smile twisting at his lips. She stood on her toes and kissed him. Her pressure lasted only for a moment before she shoved gently him after the others.

"You win this time, Red." She circled around the side of the tower and touched a thimble and fungal extension to her ear. Leoten watched her pass out of sight, then ran after the others, boots splashing in the icy seawater.

As he ran, the airborne locust circled toward him. A heavy machine gun mounted on the manta-shaped creature's underside opened fire, but at such range and in such motion, the bullets hit nothing but water. Small eruptions of cold spray flew with each impact. Leoten caught up with Viv and the three magi at the pile boat. He clambered on board as the locust circled around for another pass. His memory of the events below drew his attention for a moment, but there was nothing he could do.

· · · ·

CHAPTER 15

Leoten staggered up the metallic, ridged steps to the command center of the light cruiser. Blood pulsed from his mangled right shoulder. He turned to where the unformed captain stood behind the helm. "Make your anti-air weapons ready for an armed Locust and get us moving, captain."

The captain grimaced, obviously unhappy to simply relay orders on his ship. He saw the situation they were in, though, and repeated Leoten's words to the helmsmen and the rest of the bridge crew. Viv and Maia took Volo below to get medical attention. Nerida stayed on the command bridge close to Leoten.

"We're almost free," she said. "Thanks to you, Red."

Damaia appeared at the doorway that led from the bridge to the officers' quarters. Her wrinkled, patrician mouth curved into a smile. "Welcome back, Red. Mission accomplished."

"Yeah," he murmured. "Mission accomplished."

The dragon in his mind offered a croon of some music only he could hear, the meaning of which he didn't try to guess. The image of Aunwe swam into his mind. They'd meet again, and soon.

The visage of Hargruss reappeared as well, unbidden, amid waves of nausea. The demon might still be out there, but for now, the agencies of Drufan and the Triumvirate had beaten him. The black rod they'd brought aboard required study by other magi. For now, Leoten could rest, but his dreams would be uneasy.

The ship's engines rumbled to drive them away from Idraster. Damaia nodded to the captain. He barked a short-coded command to his crew. "Venom divine."

"Smite," answered the executive officer and then repeated the captain's words into a speaking tube.

Nerida glanced at Leoten. "What are they doing?"

He knew the Triumvirate's standard short-code orders. Venom divine meant—

The main guns boomed as they opened fire. The sound of a distant explosion from the direction of Idraster base followed a moment later.

"Why did you do that?" Nerida glared at the captain. "There are still prisoners on that base. You're killing innocent test subjects."

Damaia folded her arms. "Understand this, Magus Enn. When I'm handed an order, I don't question it. I expect all my people to do the same."

Nerida seethed as the ship fired one more volley. Tears ran down her cheeks. Leoten met Damaia's gaze but said nothing to either woman. *What words meant anything now? Honor? Compassion? Reason?* None of them mattered to the generals of the Triumvirate.

A single sentence in his report would be the most complaint he could lodge with any safety. He turned from his handler to Nerida and leaned close to her. "I'm sorry."

"You did your part, Agent Red," said Damaia.

Nerida nodded. "Don't look to me for forgiveness. I have none to give."

Leoten wondered if the bombardment would be able to kill Hargruss. He hoped Roy and Sarah had found a way out in time. The team sent with Hargruss might escape or not, but he'd lose no sleep over them either way. The lives he knew told a different story. He only hoped those tales didn't end here.

• • • •

THE STORY CONTINUES in Iron Dragon Book 3, "The Fiend Network," coming soon.

Thanks for reading.

Other Fantasy Series By Tim Niederriter

The Bondmage Series

The Demon Hunter Series

The Shifter Empire Series

ABOUT THE AUTHOR

Tim Niederriter loves writing fantasy blended with science fiction. He lives in the green valley of southern Minnesota where he plays some of the nerdiest tabletop games imaginable.

If you meet him, remember, his name is pronounced "Need a writer."

Milton Keynes UK
Ingram Content Group UK Ltd.
UKHW011113280823
427620UK00004B/394